IN THIS BED OF SNOWFLAKES WE LIE

SOPHIA SOAMES

Copyright © 2019 Sophia Soames

Second edition 2021

All rights reserved. No part of this book may be reproduced in any form or by any electronic or mechanical means, including information storage and retrieval systems, without permission in writing from the publisher, except by reviewers, who may quote brief passages in a review.

Paperback ISBN 9781701471290
Hardcover ISBN 9798325051722

Cover Artwork Copyright ©2019 Miriam Latu Instagram@om_hundre_ar_er_allting

The people in the cover images are Models and should not be connected to the Characters in the book. Any resemblance is incidental. Cover photography by Joelle Cowley. Model George Cowley.

All photos and fonts are licenced and/or free for commercial use by Sophia Soames, for distribution via electronic media and/or print. Final copy and promotional rights included.

Cover design by Aurelia Morris

Graphics: Christmas snowflake by ProSymbols from the Noun Project

This is a work of fiction. Names, characters, places and incidents are products of the Author's imagination or are used fictitiously.

References to real people, events, organisations, establishments, or locations are intended to provide a sense of authenticity and are used fictitiously. Any resemblance to actual events, locations, organisations or persons living or dead is entirely coincidental.

The Author acknowledges the copyrighted or trademarked status and trademark owners of the products mentioned in this work.

Edited by Debbie McGowan

Proofreading by Alex Korent

This book contains material that is intended for a mature adult audience. It contains graphic language, explicit sexual content and adult situations.

Find Sophia Soames on Social Media @sophiasoames

IN This BED of SNOWFLAKES we LIE

✶

SOPHIA SOAMES

Synopsis

Oskar Høiland hides from life. It just makes things easier that way, not having to face all the fears and drama of living. He avoids other people, because Oskar has grown up fearing the snide remarks and the quick glances that strip him of the tiny scraps of confidence he still has left. He is just going to keep existing. Work hard to complete his medical degree and perhaps watch a few more series on Netflix in peace and quiet over Christmas.

Erik Nøst Hansen should be an almost fully-fledged adult. He should be able to sort out the mess that festers in his head and stop lying. It's just hard. And it's bloody terrifying to even acknowledge the thoughts that swirl around in his head at night when he can't sleep. He also needs to figure out how to talk to the boy downstairs. The one with the golden curls and the crooked smile. The boy who is completely monopolising Erik's messed-up heart.

A story of falling in love and being brave. A Christmas tale with a difference, set in the university dorms of central Oslo, where lies are uncovered, snowflakes are falling all over the place, and beds are

Synopsis

made to lie in. There is a slightly unconventional family. A mess of animal onesies. Too much food and a very Merry Christmas.

SOPHIA
SOAMES

For L and M

Please note:

This story takes place in Norway, where university dorms are mixed and students are housed together with no importance placed on gender, what they study or which year they are in. You apply for housing and simply get offered the first vacant room on the list.

You are not expected to share rooms, but can apply for a single room, a double for a couple, or a family apartment for students bringing a family.

This story mentions several Norwegian brand names and food items, like gløgg, a spiced mulled wine, and julebrus, a festive soft drink. Brunost is a popular sweet whey cheese. Scandinavians are great bakers, and a traditional Christmas feast will include several kinds of homemade biscuits, pastries, sweets and bakery items.

❄

Trigger warnings: Anxiety, OCD. In chapter 26 there is a brief off page mention of Cancer, suicidal thoughts and the death of a parent. No further warnings, apart from a high risk of cravings for gingerbread biscuits.

ONE

Oskar Høiland counts himself as lucky, having ended up in Dorm 212:A. Very lucky. He is well aware how easily fate could have placed him somewhere else on campus—one of those party dorms full of pretty, popular girls and successful, confident, sporty types with opinions and attitudes, and…let's just say he thanks his lucky stars or guardian angel or whoever intervened and chose this dorm for his stint at medical school.

This ground-floor dorm, with its yellow, washed-out curtains, chipped furniture and wall-to-wall grey lino hosts a ten-bedroomed, shared corridor, a soul-destroyingly dull common room and a kitchen whose cabinets are adorned with years' worth of scrawny, scribbled names and torn-off labels left by students claiming their space, trying to protect their food and belongings from thieving, desperate hands. Well, mostly from fellow poor lazy students who wouldn't think twice about stealing a handful of pasta or a tin of chopped tomatoes from their cohabiting humans.

Oskar should hate it, but instead, he kind of effortlessly exists with the rest of the misfits who inhabit 212:A, despite his noodles regularly going missing, and he hasn't seen his favourite coffee mug for weeks. The university dorms are old, tired and in desperate need of refurbishment, but they are central to the city and cheap, and Oskar was lucky to land himself a room here. At least it's quiet and peaceful and mostly free from drama—usually, that is.

Because tonight, 212:B, the dorm upstairs, is hosting the Christmas party of the century. Rap music blasting through the ceilings of 212:A, to the point that the walls are vibrating and Oskar's desk lamp is wobbling precariously with every beat. There must be at least a hundred people jumping up and down in time to the music, and even Oskar's super-expensive, noise-cancelling headphones can't drown out what sounds like a disco warzone upstairs.

Upstairs.

Dorm 212:B is the stuff of Oskar's nightmares. The occupants of the ten rooms upstairs are a bunch of seriously cool dudes. Tough, hard-faced males who dress like the guys on MTV, slick and effortlessly handsome with bandanas and hoodies and attitudes and winning smiles, and they honestly scare the shit out of Oskar.

He doesn't think he's the only one, though, because Naomi, who barely leaves the dorm as it is, squeaks in panic if one of them passes her in the hallway, Madeleine hasn't even attempted to get to know them, which is so unlike her, since she's one of those people who talks to anyone and knows everyone. Even Freddie, the confident fourth year who dyes his hair every colour of the rainbow, champions the right to love whomever you love and doesn't give a crap what people think about him avoids them like the plague. He calls them *the plastic boys,* saying they are so slick he wouldn't need lube to get it on with them.

Not that he wants to *shag any of the little hipster boys,* Freddie always insists with his signature eye-roll and hand on hip. Despite his amateur dramatics, like Oskar, Freddie visibly shudders at the thought of the shiny creatures with questionable attitudes inhabiting 212:B, where sexual partners come and go and half-dressed humans do the walk of shame, sneaking down the concrete stairs in the early hours, with a giggle and a wave as Oskar leaves for his morning run.

Right now, there seem to be hundreds of willing sexual partners upstairs if you go by the sounds coming from the stairwell outside—squeals and pants and laughter from people getting busy. Everyone is at it—in the stairwell, on the balcony. There are even people making out in the bicycle shelter outside Oskar's window. He slams the curtains shut. Everyone is getting laid tonight.

Except Oskar. No one ever shags Oskar. Because Oskar isn't like everyone else.

He doesn't know how to speak to people, and it's not for lack of trying. He's just not very good at it, and these days, he doesn't really want to. People don't like him, and if he's honest, he rarely likes people back. That's the way it is. He never made friends at school, and the ones he thought were his friends always ended up laughing at him behind his back. He never understood why—well, maybe he did. He never wore the right clothes or rode the right bike or had the fancy trainers you were supposed to have. And people were cruel. Kids. Teenagers. Grown-ups. He was always happier on his own, in the safety of his childhood room, with his books and films and music.

Things haven't changed much now he is well into his twenties. People still disappoint him, so he chooses his own company. Solitude suits him, and 212:A is all about solitude.

The dorm is, as always, deserted on a Friday night, the doors to the bedrooms all closed, except for Naomi's down by the end. There's this unspoken rule with the doors. Open door means *come talk to me*. Closed door means *leave me alone*. People follow the rules down here, despite being a mixed bag of first to fourth years with a few mature students thrown into the mix. Oskar follows the rules too and leaves his door permanently closed. Not that anyone will come and see him, which is just the way he likes it.

He needs to check on Naomi, though, especially with the commotion going on upstairs, which will trigger her anxiety. From the acrid smell of bleach that makes his nostrils twitch, he knows exactly where he'll find her.

The common room is pristine, the twinkling lights over the windows casting a little Christmas cheer over the otherwise bleak room, the sofa deserted and the chairs around the kitchen table neatly stacked upside down on the table. The floor is gleaming wet, and Naomi is on all fours, scrubbing imaginary stains from the lino. There is nothing there, Oskar knows, because they all keep the kitchen immaculate, most of them knee-deep-in-murky-medicine students and already professionally damaged from growing bacteria on Agar plates in Lab work class during their first term.

Oskar would happily eat his morning porridge straight off the floor. Seriously. There is not a single bacterium worth its name living a healthy existence anywhere near 212:A.

He knows what Naomi is doing. He is good at reading her by now, having lived here for over a year. She's freaked out, terrified, anxious as hell, which results in epic, unstoppable cleaning frenzies until either she exhausts herself or someone manages to calm her enough to make her stop, then hides her away and soothes her racing mind until the world is a quieter, kinder place where she can slow her thoughts and feel safe again.

"Naomi."

He keeps his voice calm and soft, sitting carefully on his haunches next to her, silently swearing as the bleachy water penetrates his socks. *Damn.*

"Staphylococcus bacteria breeds easily when we have the heating on so high all through the day. It's all over the floor. I can sense it. It's everywhere."

She barely acknowledges him, scrubbing the floor with increased frenzy, her jet-black hair bunched into a messy topknot with a few loose strands stuck to her forehead.

"Naomi, it smells like a swimming pool in here. With all the bleach on the floor, there will not be a single staphylococcus bacterium left alive. I promise. Remember, I passed Bacterial Infections at one hundred per cent last term. I know my shit."

"I know you did. You pass everything one hundred per cent. You don't even have to try. You just turn up and the tutors give you full marks. Just like that." Naomi huffs and puffs with every word, continuing to sweep her sponge across the floor in front of her and splashing bleachy water over her jumper.

"You need to wear gloves. Please, let me sort out your hands and I will let you get back to cleaning."

"I *need* to finish it. Need to keep busy to drown out the noise," she groans, still not looking up from the floor. "I used to be normal. I used to party all the time, go out, have fun. I used to have a boyfriend…" She scrubs even harder.

Oskar knows this story—the one they don't mention if they know what's good for them, and for Naomi, who will go into a screaming fit of obscenities at the bare mention of her ex. Some dick called Haakon, who ruined Naomi's life and took her sanity with him when he fucked off to Australia or wherever he now parks his arse at night and makes the world a dark place around him. All according to Naomi.

"Can't stop. Oh, no—my hands!"

The skin is tight and an angry red. Her obsessive handwashing and cleaning aggravates her dermatitis, and the creases in her already-mangled hands are seeping with tiny streaks of blood as she holds them up in front of her.

Oskar has done this before. Not only is dermatology something he has studied, but he also understands Naomi. He gets why she does what she does. Understands how she feels. Fuck, he's pretty much like her himself, except that he spits out his obsessions through his impossible perfectionism in his studies, the daily runs that he needs to rein in, and his quirk for keeping his room in a constant state of absolute despair.

Unquestionably, Oskar Høiland is a loser. A nerd of the first degree. A friendless, partnerless idiot who, at the ancient age of twenty-two, hasn't been laid. Or been kissed. Or been anywhere close to getting laid or kissed for that matter. He hasn't even held anyone's hand, for God's sake. Well, apart from Naomi's, as he slowly leads her across the sloshy floor to the sink so he can rinse her hands under the warm water from the tap.

"Let me take care of your hands, Naomi. Just breathe with me."

She tries, but her breaths are ragged and frenzied, her eyes closed as she winces with pain. She's done this before—fucked up her hands with bleach, too lost in her need to follow her instincts to notice the skin cracking between her fingers. Too full of her anxious thoughts to realise she should stop. Oskar understands. He knows. This isn't the first time, and it won't be the last.

The cupboard marked with his name is next to them, and he rummages around between the packets to find the tube of cream he left there for times like this. Thick, gloopy ointment that he carefully slathers over her broken skin. Soft movements of his fingers over hers.

"Let's sit," he whispers and guides her towards the sofa, crouching in front of her as she sits, her hands still cradled in his as he softly massages the cream into her damaged skin. The motion seems to calm her and hopefully soothes the angry red still visible through the layers of Vaseline and calming oils.

"Stay here. I need to open the front door for a few minutes, so I can get some air in here."

The fumes are making him dizzy, but the stress of the noise from upstairs is not helping, and there's a bunch of people talking and laughing outside the window, which he slams shut after inhaling a mouthful of their tobacco smoke carried in with the cold draught.

What he and Naomi need right now, more than fresh air, is peace and quiet. A moment of silence so he can help her get back in control. He feels like banging on a few doors to get some back-up. Not that Ingrid or Madeleine would help clean up Naomi's mess, they would just stand there and roll their eyes and bitch about their socks getting ruined. The thought prompts Oskar to take off his own soaked excuse for socks and throw them in the bin on his way out.

His angry-pink bare feet slap against the cool lino as he tiptoes down the hall to the front door, which he wedges open with a weather-eroded brick someone must have left outside years ago for that sole purpose. The icy December wind batters him relentlessly as he hops back over the threshold, his thin T-shirt and rolled-up jeans offering no protection. He should get a jumper from his room. He should go wash his feet. Instead, he grabs the dry mop from the cleaning cupboard and returns to the common room, where he sloshes the water around, leaving Naomi on the sofa with her now bare feet up underneath her, her wet socks in a puddle on the floor and her hands resting gently on her lap.

She looks distraught. Jumpy and nervous as the beat changes and at least fifty people bounce to the tune blasting out above them. It's deafening. Exhausting.

"Shall I take Naomi?" a voice from behind asks quietly.

Oskar turns to find Freddie watching her with that concerned look he always gets around her as he figures out what state she's in —if it's one of the days when she stands tall and flashes that brilliant smile of hers or one when she's broken into so many little pieces, she can barely function.

"Don't let her wash her hands," Oskar whispers back, the textbook pseudo-doctor who thinks he knows best when in reality he knows fuck all. Because seriously, he doesn't. He doesn't understand the world. He doesn't understand his family. He doesn't know how to make friends. He can't comprehend how people fall in love—how the whole romance thing works. Fuck, he doesn't even understand himself.

Leaving Naomi in Freddie's capable, caring hands, he slips his headphones back on and drowns out the world by blasting NWA so loudly he's pretty sure he's doing permanent damage to his eardrums, while he mops up bleach-laden water and empties bucket after bucket into the sink.

The chairs get shoved back under the table and the bucket and mop get thrown back into the cleaning cupboard to the tune of American explicit rap lines and deep bass rhythms. Slamming the front door shut with an angry kick, he stumbles awkwardly backwards as the bitter wind slaps his face. It's so fucking cold, he can barely feel his feet.

The sounds from upstairs seem duller as he takes his headphones off and closes the door to his dorm room. His little sanctuary. His home. His safe space where he can breathe, away from all the pressure of having to be something he's not. He doesn't have to pretend in here. *This is just Oskar, in all his nerdy glory*, he thinks as he strips off and steps into the shower, feeling his body slowly heat back up under the hot jets. He lets his mind wander for once, hoping he can find something on Netflix to distract him from the world before bed. Something to relax him enough that he can sleep.

Naked as the day he was born, he steps back into the dusky light from his desk lamp, towel drying his hair with one hand and with the other tapping his laptop screen to power it back up. The mirror on the wall reflects his body in all its…well…Oskar snickers to himself. He's not built or muscular, but he's defined from his daily running and slim because he can't be bothered to cook most of the time.

He looks okay. He's not butt ugly. His hair is a mess of long, blond curls because when he cuts it, he looks like a freak, all angles and edges. As it is, his hair frames his face. Despite his dad's humorous digs that he'll never get a job with a haircut like that, he likes the way the long strands add another layer of protection—something else he can hide behind. Hide the skin that is mottled with scars and faded acne, the nose that the rest of his features never grew into. He's plain. Nothing special. One of those faces that blends into the background. Rarely noticed and never remembered.

Christmas star, he thinks. *I should buy a Christmas star to hang in the window. Or one of those arched electric candle holders, just something to make it a bit festive in here. Homely. Cosy.*

He has nothing on the walls. His desk is covered in reference books and paperwork, the floor littered with charging cables and rubbish that he really should gather up and throw in the bin. He's pretty sure there are old pizza boxes under the bed, plates long forgotten lurking in the corners.

The light from the laptop casts the room in bluish light as Oskar lifts it up and turns around, ready to tumble onto his bed. It's the only luxury he brought from his childhood home—the super-duper, mega-comfy, king-sized bed his dad bought for his fifteenth birthday. It seemed such a crazy present at the time, like his dad was hinting that he was growing up and might one day have someone to share his bed with. Nudge, nudge. Wink, wink.

But the oversized bed has only ever had the pleasure of hosting Oskar. There has never been a single other human being in it. Which is freaking him out now, as he stands staring at what's in front of him.

Because Oskar's bed is *not* empty. There *is* another human being in it. A *very tall* human being, wearing an enormous black hoodie and a pink bandana tied around his forehead.

TWO

Oskar's first instinct is to flee, hide somewhere until the thing in his bed disappears. He blinks, shakes his head in disbelief and looks again.

Nope. There is still a very-much-fast-asleep person in his bed, breathing softly against the pillow—*Oskar's* pillow—and that outlandish pink bandana is sliding down over his eyes.

Oskar moves carefully, then freezes as he remembers. *No clothes!* He is stark naked in his own room, like a normal person would be. Except…this dude is here too. Right here. On his bed.

Yes, he left his door unlocked, but that doesn't mean any random person can just come in and decide to sleep in his bed, does it? Especially when the random person is flat-out drunk. Oskar can smell the alcohol and recoils at the little bubbles of spit dribbling from the corner of the dude's mouth, beer-scented breath escaping with every snore.

How did he not realise someone was here before? The dude is hardly quiet, snuffling and smacking his lips in his sleep. Oskar's ears are still ringing from having his music on the highest volume, and the beats from upstairs are still going strong. Even so, he should have noticed. How the fuck didn't he notice?

Spotting a pair of his threadbare joggers on the floor, he pulls them on, and that T-shirt looks clean enough, so he tugs it over his damp hair, feeding his arms into the sleeves as he tiptoes along the side of his bed to get a closer look.

It's definitely one of the guys from upstairs. The tall, good-looking one with the messy, dark-brown hair and full lips. The one with all the girlfriends. The one with the reputation.

Yes, Oskar listens. He might not speak much to the other students, but his hearing is good—well, it was until today, and he will sue if his hearing is damaged from that bloody party, starting with suing the pants off the dude who's interrupted his planned Netflix marathon—and he pays attention to the stories. The tall tales of weekend shenanigans, the obvious boasting and lies…and the things that might actually be true.

Like the whispers doing the rounds about this guy. Kisses like he means it. Great lay, apparently. Can get any girl he wants. That's what Oskar's heard. Hangs around with the dark-haired guy with the floppy black fringe and that lanky boy with the frizzy hair. Well, he probably hangs around with *everyone*. Always smiling, never alone. Never sitting on his own in the cafeteria like Oskar, hiding in the corner with his headphones on.

No, this dude is always the centre of attention, surrounded by people hanging on his every word, laughing at his jokes and staring adoringly at him.

Except now he's here, and Oskar hasn't got a clue what to do.

He could go get Freddie, he supposes, and they could probably manhandle the dude out of the room, dump him in the common room for the night. He's quite sure the girls would approve, other than Naomi, of course, and in the morning, Oskar would wake up and find this guy on the sofa making all the girls laugh, having charmed them into getting him coffee and spoon-feeding him their secret imported stash of Swedish Treo hangover fizz while placing tiny morsels of hot, buttered toast on his tongue.

Oskar pushes that scene out of his head with a sigh. The boy is *his* problem. He is in *Oskar's* bed, and if he doesn't get him out of here, things will be shit awkward in the morning, he is sure of that.

"Dude," he whispers and nudges the guy's shoulder before he can stop himself. He should think this through, make some kind of plan. Maybe wake him up gently so Oskar doesn't scare the shit out of the poor guy when he realises where he's crashed. He probably took a wrong turn, thinking this was Madeleine's or Ingrid's or one of the other girls' rooms. Maybe he thought he could get lucky by throwing himself in some random girl's bed. Oskar wonders if people do that, just full-on go for it and shamelessly offer themselves.

He shudders at the thought. It's a mistake, whatever, and

Oskar won't let him get away with this. Not tonight. Not now. He doesn't need the grief or the inevitable shaming when this dude tells all his friends that the nerd downstairs tried to get him in the sack, all the lies and raw laughter with Oskar as the butt of every joke. Then he'd be the one the girls gossiped about and pointed their fingers at, for coming on to one of the beautiful people—*their* people.

Because the boy is *beautiful*, even Oskar can see that. Soft, long, dark hair frames his face; freckles decorate his pale skin. Those luscious lips. Even his striking profile is perfect—the straight nose, that defined jawline…those lips…

"Dude, come on! Wake up!" Oskar shakes the guy's shoulder this time, but he's dead to the world. He doesn't even stir, just snores and burrows further into the pillow.

"YO! MATE!" This guy is no mate of his. Nor will they ever be mates, but Oskar is desperate to get to bed. He needs an hour of some mindless American sitcom to calm him down. He needs to sleep. Please.

He tries to pull the guy off the bed, grabbing him by the ankles, only to realise the guy is still wearing shoes. Big, clumsy boots with heels. Ridiculous! Who wears shit like that in the middle of winter? They might be all right for a Texas rodeo, but December in Oslo is not the place for those boots.

"Fuck," he grits between his teeth.

The sofa out in the main room is seriously uncomfortable, and smells of dust and years of spilled foods. Even if it was comfortable enough to sleep on, the bleach fumes still lingering in the air would have Oskar retching before too long. But it's not like he can go sleep in anyone else's room. It's just not the kind of thing he could do. Not that he is close enough to any of the others to warrant such a request.

He could sleep on his own floor, he supposes, except his duvet is trapped under the goddamn snoring trespasser.

It takes a few good pulls, but finally, the guy rolls over and Oskar drags the fabric out from underneath him, then almost bursts into laughter because the dude is now on his back, mouth wide open, and the bandana has slipped down covering his eyes and nose. He looks like a dickhead.

A drunk, snoring dickhead wearing inappropriate boots.

Oskar is a medical student so he knows what can happen. He wouldn't be a responsible human being if he didn't ensure his unwelcome roommate at least survives the night.

The boots come off to reveal socks with little reindeer and Santas, and Oskar swallows another inappropriate giggle because this isn't funny. This isn't funny at all.

He rolls the bandana up over the dude's fringe, easing it off the top of his head before tossing it aside, and straddles his body to try to roll him into the recovery position. He has done this several times in training but always with willing and perfectly conscious subjects underneath him, never a half-dead drunk huffing alcohol fumes in his face.

It takes a few goes, and Oskar gets braver, as the guy is definitely out for the count. He doesn't wake up, even when Oskar accidentally knees him in the balls, trying to manhandle his shoulder over towards the mattress. But he is finally there, safely in position on his side with his hand supporting his chin, so any vomiting won't choke him to death, and there's nothing around his neck to hinder his breathing. His airway is open, and he is safe. In the middle of Oskar's bed.

Oskar wants to cry. He wants to bury his face in his hands and howl in frustration.

Instead, he covers the unconscious body in his warm duvet and switches off the light, then slides himself in under the covers, keeping as far away as he can. Balanced on the edge of the mattress, he still feels the soft puffs of breath stroking the skin under his still-damp hair.

It's hours until he finally falls asleep, his mind restless and terrified of what he might find next to him in the morning. Wound up to the point that he lets himself laugh out loud at the absurdity of the whole situation. He sleeps, thinking anything but this, would be a welcome relief.

THREE

Erik needs to curtail his drinking. Not that he has a problem. Oh no. It's just when he gets like he got last night. He was out of control, letting things get on top of him. He needs to find a way to rein himself in when he can't figure shit out, instead of drowning his panic in copious amounts of alcohol.

It's totally out of hand, and look where it's got him. Here. On a Sunday morning with the worst headache in the history of headaches.

There's normally a packet of Paracet tucked in his bedside table, and he reaches out to open the drawer only to smash his hand into something solid and wince in pain like a child.

"Who freaking moved my bedside table?" He rolls over so he can feel for the water bottle he keeps next to his bed, and— *Wall.* His nose is now wedged up against a wall. Was he really that drunk last night that he rearranged his furniture in a drunken stupor? At least his bedding is clean, smelling softly of washing powder and…*ugh*. He catches a mouthful of his own morning breath and almost hurls. *Fuck.*

Sitting up is too painful. His brain has obviously detached from his skull again, causing flashes of light to painfully dart across his vision as he tries to open his eyes. The curtains are shut. *Thank God.*

He still catches sight of a desk and covers his eyes with both hands, trying to get his vision under control.

"What the fuck?"

Someone has stolen his desktop. Both screens and his drawing pad. Fuck, someone has stolen the lot. All his shit. And replaced his freaking unreplaceable, state-of-the-art graphics setup with a weird cheap looking laptop. Not only that, but there's a lamp he doesn't recognise and… He lets his eyes dart around the room.

The curtains are the same cheap, washed-out yellow cotton ones that the university housing society must have bought in bulk, as most dorm rooms have them, and the desk is the same, but the rest? This is not his room. Fuck.

At least he's alone in the bed, and he desperately racks his brain as to where he could be. He can't remember hooking up with anyone last night, and he's pretty sure he locked up his room before people started to arrive. It's all good and well hosting epic parties, but the morning after, Erik likes to wake up in his own bed and with most of his life intact. Which doesn't seem to be the case this morning.

He's also still dressed. He sighs and fumbles awkwardly with his hoodie. He hates sleeping in his clothes, and now he's noticed, he feels overheated and nauseous. His arms get stuck when he tries to pull the hoodie over his head, and by the time he's fought his way out of it, he's hyperventilating. He launches the offending, sweat-drenched jumper away from him and watches it slide down the wall at the end of the bed.

The end of the bed. Fuck. There are a pair of legs standing there, muscular, shiny legs in spandex running gear, leading up to…
Oh fuck.

"Disney Prince," Erik mutters and falls back against the pillows. Because of course. Of course it would have to be him. How the hell did *he* end up here?

"What?" the Disney Prince says. To be honest, he looks terrified, like Erik is a full-blown vampire-werewolf-shifter monster or a bloodthirsty zombie.

And to be very honest, Erik feels like death warmed up and is about to go into a long rant about how he isn't a zombie even though he does feel like one, and if he could join the world of the undead, he would probably fit right in, in his current state.

"What did you call me?" the Disney Prince hisses. He looks hacked off, like Erik is intentionally winding him up when he is not. No. Erik is dying, mortified with embarrassment.

"I'm sorry. Didn't mean to say that out loud." It's a poor excuse for an apology. He knows that. But he can't run in the state he's in, however much he would love to get up and push past the man in front of him and disappear, never set foot in this part of the campus again. What the hell was he thinking?

"I don't appreciate you mocking me. I don't appreciate people crashing in my room. I've barely slept all night, and I am…" The Disney Prince waves his arms about, then pulls at his hair and stomps around. He's put out. That's clear.

"I don't know how I ended up here," Erik lies. He knows full well how he ended up here. He was pissed out of his head and didn't know what the hell he was. Well, he did, but not in a good sensible way.

"You live upstairs, don't you? How the hell can you end up in the wrong bloody dorm on the wrong floor? I mean…" The Disney Prince is pacing the room now, his hair drenched in sweat and his face flushed. "I went for a run an hour ago, and I expected to come back and find you gone. I gave you an out. Just fuck the hell out of here!"

Well, fuck me, Erik thinks. The Disney Prince has a temper, although he seems horrified by the profanities spilling out of his mouth, and he has that terrified, singlehandedly-fighting-the-zombie-apocalypse look on his face again.

"Can you give me an hour? Please. I can't face walking at the moment. You don't happen to have any Panodil? Paracet? Ibux? Anything? I'm dying here." Erik is. At least that bit's true.

Not only is he crashing in the Disney Prince's room, he's also demanding to stay like some deranged diva with delusions of grandeur who thinks he's entitled to someone else's painkillers.

His spandex-wearing adversary seems to have run out of steam and is sat on the edge of the chair by the desk, hunched over with his head in his hands. It's some consolation he hasn't planted a fist in Erik's mouth nor laughed in his face. *Yet*. It's only a matter of time though, because Erik isn't an easy guy to have around. He's impulsive and over the top and intense and needy and demanding.

The Disney Prince honestly looks like he wants to cry. He also needs a shower. There is a seriously bad stench of sweat wafting through the room, and it's not just his.

"I'll make it up to you," Erik promises. "I can owe you a favour.

Please. Just give me an hour." He can't even look at the guy, his face buried in the pillow. "Your bed is awesome, by the way. Best bed ever. Epic. If I was your girlfriend, I would never leave."

He's talking a load of shit again, and if he didn't know better, he'd have sworn the Disney Prince let a giggle escape.

"No girlfriend," the guy says calmly.

"Boyfriend?" Erik counters. In this day and age, you should be open and accepting. Inclusive. Kind. Though he's still face down in the pillows and not sure he wants to know the answer.

"No." The Disney Prince laughs. "Total loser, me."

"Don't believe you." Erik rolls over and half sits up, then immediately regrets it and falls back into the pillow again with a groan.

"You're really suffering, aren't you?" The guy's voice is surprisingly calm.

"You're the doctor, you tell me."

"Not a doctor. Medicine student. Second year."

"Good enough. Don't suppose you've figured out how to diagnose and cure someone dying of a hangover?" Erik tries to turn it into a joke, but his head is a mess and his thoughts are scrambled, and right now sleep would be fantastic—after a heavenly cocktail of water and painkillers.

"I don't really drink or party, as such, so I wouldn't know. But you stink like a brewery and look like death. I kind of get that." The Disney Prince sighs and rummages in one of his desk drawers. Erik flinches at the banging and scraping.

There are footsteps and doors opening and closing, echoes from the corridor outside, and voices talking. Soft laughter and the sound of the door handle moving again before the bed dips next to him and a hand grabs his arm, tugging at him to sit up.

"Come on you, let's get some paracetamol into you. Here." Fingers press bitter-tasting pills against his lips, and he greedily gulps down the glass of water he's given, although it hurts too much to sit up. As he lies back down, the glass is removed from his, tenuous, shaking grip.

"Thank you," he whispers as he curls up and hands tuck the duvet back up over his shoulders.

"What did you call me earlier? The Dizzy Prince? Why?" The guy sounds amused, not so hostile.

"The Disney Prince. We have nicknames for all of you, and that's yours. The Disney Prince." Erik's eyes are heavy. He can't even think straight now. He wants to sleep. And listen to that soothing voice next to him.

"Why on earth would you call me that? Is it supposed to be some kind of joke?" He seems more confused than angry. Maybe a little irritated.

"Because you look like a Disney Prince. If I was making a film with a prince in it, he would look just like you."

The guy says something back, Erik thinks. He feels the mattress move and then hears footsteps retreating. He doesn't remember anything else, just that he is warm and safe and comfortable. And asleep. He is definitely asleep.

FOUR

It's not often Oskar gets people wrong. He has become good at reading people, knowing when to duck and when to dive.

And when it is safe to speak.

Normally, he would never, ever have dared to speak to any of the guys upstairs. They are the kind of people Oskar remembers from school. Short-sighted, quick to judge, the kind who put others down with words and glances so they themselves can feel bigger, better and cooler than the rest of the world.

Oskar has spent his life hiding from people like the guys upstairs. Until today. Because the guy in his bed is a hungover mess, but he seems okay. Or maybe he's okay with Oskar because he's kind of trapped in Oskar's bed and realises it's easier for once if he doesn't behave like a total jerk. Not that Oskar expects the guy to remember the favour he now owes him, like whether he promises not to trip Oskar up on the stairs or steal his bike in return for the hour's sleep in Oskar's bed.

He does agree about the bed being epic, though. Those are proper feather-filled fluffy pillows and a duck down duvet—another birthday present from his dad, and with 1000-thread count Egyptian cotton sheets. The fact his dad works for one of the top bed manufacturing companies in Scandinavia accounts for some of that, and he knows his stuff, but he's pretty awesome too.

Parents are parents, and Oskar knows he's been lucky with his. They might not be perfect, but they do love him. On the rare occasions he visits, his mum treats him like an adult and his dad gives him space. They show an appropriate amount of interest in his studies and pop the occasional joke about Oskar finding himself a girlfriend. It's cool. Oskar can cope with that. Still, coming back to the safety of his dorm room where he can close the door and breathe is the best feeling in the world.

Except today, when he is not alone. Not safe. Not in any way safe or calm.

He pops his head around the corner and checks on the guy in his bed. Still asleep, with most of the duvet bunched up in his arms like he's clinging to an oversized teddy bear. His nose is buried in the fabric, and there are soft snores escaping his mouth. He is totally out of it.

Nevertheless, Oskar locks his bathroom door—better safe than sorry. He had an extra-long run this morning and hasn't eaten, so he's dithering and feels a bit faint. He turns on the shower and steps underneath the warm jets, trying to relax the muscles in his shoulders, which are stiff with the stress from last night. He barely slept, too aware of the body next to him and too nervous about what would happen this morning.

He got up early and slipped into his running gear, making what should have been enough noise to gently wake the dude in his bed, followed by slamming the door shut to ensure his wake-up tactic was solid. If the guy had any sense, he'd realise he was somewhere he shouldn't be and get the hell out of there before anyone noticed.

Well, that had backfired. Instead, the guy had been all cute and grumpy and called him a bloody Disney Prince. Oskar chuckles to himself. It was kind of sweet, even though he is no fairy-tale prince. Fuck that.

The towel is still wet from last night, lying in a heap on the floor, but he has no choice so wraps the damp, cold fabric around his waist before tiptoeing around his room to try to find something clean and warm to wear. It's cold, the window open a crack to vent the alcohol fumes Oskar woke up to. Despite the chilly breeze, the stale air hits the back of his throat as he checks on the sleeping man tangled up in his duvet.

Oskar pulls a sweatshirt over his head. He's cold. He's tired—freaking exhausted if he's honest—and the bed looks damn inviting, unwanted guest or not. The guy's turned around in his sleep, still hugging the bedding, and Oskar's brain is saying *go out and make some breakfast. Go out and get away.* But his body won't cooperate. He falls carelessly onto the bed, grabbing the edge of the duvet in a swift jerk, giving him just enough to cover his body. The fabric is warm against his hands. Warm and soft and…

He sleeps. He sleeps like he's dead, then he wakes up with his shoulders aching from the stiffness of not moving. He wakes up alone and warm in a bed smelling of someone else.

Oskar curls in on himself like a coiled snake until he's aching from the strain of holding on too tight. The muscles in his legs hurt from not having done his stretches properly after his morning run. His skin covered in goosebumps from trying to keep himself warm. His heart is split open like it's been sliced with a knife.

He never knew it could be like this. That just the thought of having someone sleep next to you could fill you with fear. Fill you with all these feelings.

A volcano of questions race through his thoughts until his head wants to erupt. Who the heck was that guy anyway? What if, through some strange blip in the universe, he was meant to be here? What if it wasn't a crazy accident—a fluke of some drunken madness—and Oskar just flipped him off like he's nothing, an inconvenience and a hassle?

What if he'd still been here when Oskar woke up?

His face is burning, and his eyes are wet from feelings he doesn't understand.

This is why he'll never have a working relationship, let alone friendship, with anyone. This is what is wrong with him. He doesn't 'get' other people. He never has, never will. And anyway, the thoughts filling his head are just that. Stupid, reckless fantasies that will never, ever come to fruition in any shape or form. The guy is not into Oskar, and Oskar is definitely not into…guys like that. What*ever*.

At least he has his room back, he thinks as he stretches uncomfortably and rolls out of bed. His legs go all Bambi on him, and his hands shake uncontrollably as his blood sugar crashes. Who is he kidding? It crashed hours ago. He can barely function as he hobbles out into the common room, wearing his threadbare dressing gown and mismatching socks, and makes a beeline for the coffee maker, saying a little prayer in gratitude to whoever left the lukewarm dribble of coffee in the pot for him to find.

"Look who's rolled out of bed. Finally." Carolina is perched on the sofa, laptop in front of her and a mug of coffee in her hand.

"I didn't sleep very well last night," Oskar lies. "Noise and all that." He gestures with his hand, lamely pointing to the ceiling while downing the coffee in one and topping up his cup with the last drops.

"I'll put another pot on for you," Carolina says as she gets up and shuffles over in her giant novelty slippers. Unicorns today—white and fluffy with giant, phallic horns on the front. Quite obscene, Oskar thinks.

"Why are you being nice to me today? What do you want? Lost your notes from that gastro-intestinal lecture again?" He knows he sounds snarky as hell, but Carolina is safe. She always has been. She's loud and direct and funny and doesn't give a toss. She also flirts shamelessly with him, which is kind of amusing. They both know there's nothing there. Just an easy friendship of sorts that Oskar is still trying to get his head around.

"No. I want the gossip. You know? The one time someone sneaks out of your room in the early hours of the morning, and I manage to catch him? He looked guilty as hell, by the way. Well fucked. You did good, boy. Impressed. Kudos to you, my friend, pegging a hottie." She raises her hand to high-five him, and Oskar stands there, his mouth hanging open, as all the blood in his body pools in his cheeks. Feeling a little faint, he clumsily meets Carolina's hand with his own.

"No pegging," Oskar starts, then shakes his head in frustration. "Look, nothing happened. Nothing. He's a mate. Needed a favour." His voice is a bit too loud, and his body language screaming, "Lies, *lies, LIES*!" but he can't help himself. He's not built for this shit, not when Carolina is mimicking a blow job with her hand against her lips and her tongue poking the inside of her cheek.

"Oh, yeah? I bet he did. Hot stuff." She laughs and turns away to deal with the coffee. "So, is this a thing? How long has it been going on?"

He quite expects her face to be teasing, her voice full of laughter, but when she turns his way again, she looks sincere. Happy almost.

"Nothing is going on, Carolina. Nothing!" Oskar wants to go back to his room, shut the door in everyone's face and scream into his pillows in frustration, but he needs to eat or he's going to pass out.

"Yeah, right. Well, you know, I have options. I can always go up and talk to Erik." She beams, triumphant. "I bet he'll tell me *all* the gossip. I know how to make him talk."

"Who the fuck is Erik?" Oskar screeches and rips open a packet of muesli. Extra fibre. Added Omega oils. *Honestly.* He sleeps late for a few hours and the whole world has gone crazy.

"Oskar, you're not fooling anyone. Erik. *Your* Erik. You did ask his name, didn't you? Before you let your steel-hard member slide down his willing throat." Carolina throws out the last sentence in her best theatrical voice, leaning her head back and gyrating her hips against the kitchen counter.

"Erik. Is that his name?" He laughs awkwardly. He feels like such a prick.

"Erik Nøst Hansen, Graphic Design and Media. Third year. Seriously cool dude. Can't believe you did him. I mean, have you got some kind of magical dick magnet or something? I would've let him do me. Anytime. I mean, *hello*? Have you seen those lips? Oh, yes, you have. Sorry, Oskar. Forgot. You did see them. Wrapped tightly around that cock of yours last night. Am I right?"

"Carolina. Fuck the hell off!" Oskar warns. *Seriously.* "You know nothing. Don't piss on me. I'm not in the mood."

Don't piss on me? Oskar doesn't even know where that came from, speaking like he is some kind of tough person.

"Oh, are you into a bit of waterworks? Kinky play?" Carolina throws her head back in laughter. "You surprise me, Høiland. A year and a half of living here and I was seriously thinking you were some kind of eunuch, like your dick had shrivelled up and fallen off. Then you go and surprise us all by fucking the king of the plastics up there. I *am* impressed. I'll say it again. Kudos."

"Can you just shut the fuck up?" Oskar can't take it. He just can't. It's too much, and there are stupid tears welling up in the corners of his eyes. Too many feelings and shit and fuck and then *fucking hell, Carolina.* "Just leave it. Please just leave it."

"Oh, come here. Let's hug it out." Carolina tugs at him, pulls at his arms. Lays her head against his chest and hums as she hauls him in for the most awkward hug in the history of hugs, and Oskar doesn't know shit right now.

A minute later, he huddles back under his duvet with a bowl of dry muesli. He ran without thinking. Didn't even grab the milk, and he is NOT going back out there. Not in a million years.

His head swirls all afternoon as he tries to immerse himself in his immunology case study, failing to put a single line on the screen in front of him.

The boy's name is Erik. Erik. It sits on his tongue like it belongs there, and it's messing with Oskar's head. *Erik.*

Fucking bloody Erik.

He throws himself on his bed, letting the laptop balance on his knees through half a season of some documentary on people living off the grid in bloody Alaska, before his stomach rumbles and he curls up in a ball. He needs to go for another run. It will help. Just an hour of mindless pounding against the snow-covered ground would take the edge off it all, calm the anxiety paralysing his body.

He knows he shouldn't. The rational part of his brain knows his knees are fucked and need a break. His brain also understands that he has barely eaten all day, has only drunk a cup and a splash of lukewarm coffee, and his blood sugar is dangerously low. He is tired. Dehydrated. Exhausted. Shivering in the thick hoodie he is wearing, even though he is tucked under the duvet with that pillow pressed to his chest. *The pillow Erik slept on.*

Erik. His imaginary friend. The bloke from upstairs who, in a drunken stupor, ended up spending a few hours snoring next to him. It meant nothing. It means nothing at all.

Maybe he should do what Naomi does. Get up and pour bleach all over his floor and scrub it until his knuckles bleed. Anything to make himself feel better. Anything to make himself feel less of a failure and a loser and a freak.

He needs to go out there and eat something. He needs to have a shower and go to sleep. Behave like a normal person. Drink about a litre of water in one go.

Instead, he pulls the duvet over his head and groans in frustration.

He needs to get a grip. He needs to get himself under control. Stop all these stupid fantasies that have somehow planted themselves in his head.

Erik. His name is Erik.

FIVE

Three days is all it takes before Erik breaks. Three bloody days.

He's not like this. He's honestly not. He's a good person, and yes, he teases and messes around and sometimes hurts people's feelings. Yes, he can be an arse about it, and he's broken a few people's hearts. He knows that. It's easier than trying to explain. He's so tired of trying to explain things that he can't understand himself.

The drinking is a convenient cop-out because nobody bats an eyelid if you pass out drunk in the middle of a party. They laugh at him and call him a lightweight, but it's not like he does it all the time.

He likes the kissing. He likes the snuggling and the dancing. But you have to *feel* to take it further, and Erik tends not to feel a thing. It's just skin against skin and spit and hands everywhere…until he feels like he is suffocating and he has to get out. Like there is something seriously wrong with him.

You have to want it to have sex. You have to get turned on. Get that buzz in your body that you want more.

It's not like he's a virgin, because he's had sex. Stuck his cock inside a few girls.

You're supposed to feel. You're supposed to lose your mind from the sensations of it all. Yet all he felt was numb. Numb and tired and distraught.

So, instead of dealing with it, he's an arse. He kisses and flirts and pretends he's something he is not because all he wants is to feel. Feel something real. Something he can touch and hold on to and want and need.

He kind of knows—no, scrap that. He has *always* known. And it's not like he's going to be stoned to death or jailed or beaten up for being in love with…he can't even think it, let alone make his mouth say the words.

Okay, so it hasn't really been a thing, a clear concept in his mind, until that fateful day at the beginning of term almost eighteen months ago. A normal late-summer evening after a normal whatever day it had been. This guy pushed past him in the stairwell, a tall, skinny bloke in ludicrous spandex running gear that was pretty much a second skin, and Erik stared like a deranged lunatic, because… *Yes. Wow. Legs.* Legs that went on for days. A firm arse hugged tight in those…leggings? Were they called that? Muscular arms that cast shapes and shadows through the tight fabric, and golden-blond hair that moved with every step the guy took. His hair was shorter then, cut into some kind of style, but it's longer now, looking soft to touch. Anyway, Erik stopped and stood there, staring while the guy did a few awkward-looking stretches in the failing daylight before taking a few tentative steps and setting off at an unbelievably fast pace towards the end of the road.

It shouldn't have meant anything. It was just this random dude, but Erik's heart fluttered, and his stomach filled with absurd butterflies while his mind created monsters in his head.

The next time he saw him, Erik kept his head down while his heart banged holes in his ribcage. He started to get up at ridiculous times in the mornings, hoping to catch a glimpse of golden-blond curls running down the road. He figured out the guy's routine and sat in the kitchen window with his coffee every morning at 6.37, ready to watch him run out the door.

Then he partied and made out with girls and pretended and faked it and lied, all while his mind was trying to suppress the truth swirling uncomfortably in his gut.

It's bad enough that his mum is obsessed with the whole 'free your heart' concept she waffled on about. He was raised to love. He was raised to have an open mind and an open heart. He has. He's not judging anyone, and his mum is the best. She may be all wrapped up in her own ideas and live in an ideal dreamworld, but she's right. She is always right. He needs to grow up and finally get a grip. Then he needs to once and for all do something about it. She's even made him a plan of what he should do.

It's a good one, her idea. A solid one. Now he needs to be brave and take the first step. Then follow through. He can almost hear her soft voice in his head, with that edge of laughter it always carries as the words spill out of her mouth with such ease and warmth. He is loved. He is cherished. He is so very much loved.

The other guys in his dorm must kind of know by now; he's thrown enough hints out there. And it's not like they'll look at him differently.

Nobody says anything about Adam and Mikael. Not that they rub it in anyone's faces, but come on, they sleep in Adam's room. The only time Mikael sets foot in his own room is right before exams when he needs to study, and there are the little touches, lingering just that second too long. The glances. The little smiles. The secrets they think nobody else knows, yet they're written all over their faces. These are the little things that make Erik green with envy.

Because he wants that. He wants to be loved, and have that over-the-top epic love story happen to him, where someone will fall in love with him so desperately that he won't be able to help his pathetic little heart. Yeah. It's pathetic, all right. He's not five. He's almost twenty-five, not a child waiting for the love of his life to come and rescue him out of his imaginary second-floor tower.

No one will judge him. No one will care. All the guys up here are solid, and none of them are dickheads. He knows that. Ammar keeps grabbing his shoulder and giving him that look—the one that says *get yourself together, my friend. You can do this.* And Jakob smiles at him when he sits by the kitchen window with his nose pressed against the cold glass, watching until the man in spandex speedily disappears around the corner down by the clearing. As for Victor… well, he's so lost in his head most of the time that he probably wouldn't notice if an atomic bomb was dropped on them all. Honestly.

Lastly, there's Mathias who, in all his well-meaning hopeless, clueless heart, had gallantly offered to march downstairs, throw the Disney Prince over his shoulder and deposit him on Erik's lap…if he could only stop looking like the world was about to end in the middle of their epic Christmas party.

So they all know he has a *little bit* of an obsession going on with the Disney Prince downstairs.

The prince with the golden curls who is kind to everyone. Erik watched him this morning as he ran off into the distance in that hide-nothing running gear, headphones on, his neon-striped shoes pounding the hard snow. Erik listens. Watches. Dreams. The guy is nice; everyone says so. Helpful and tidy, lends study notes and checks essays. He's apparently smart and really into fitness.

Of course, Erik being Erik, he's made up this whole adventure in his head, where the Disney Prince saves the day in a million different ways and then falls at Erik's feet to declare his undying love. Or there's the one where they accidentally bump shoulders in passing, and the Disney Prince grabs his arm and slams him into the wall, cupping his chin to home in on his lips and…

He needs to sleep if he's going to function tomorrow, and sitting here swirling in his own stupid thoughts isn't helping, whatever the outcome. He might as well go down there and make an arse of himself. After all, how bad can it be? He only wants to apologise.

Yeah, right. And crawl into bed with his prince and let everything just melt away while the man whose bed he's in stares at him, and then he will pretend he is asleep, and everything will just be awkward, but Erik can't help himself.

He sits, pathetically spinning in circles in his oversized office chair, on each spin, his unfinished assignment whizzes past his face. The colourful charts light up the room like a multicoloured disco ball on pause. There are too many colours. Too many ideas. Too much of everything. Just like Erik. His head really won't switch off.

So he showers until he feels like a boiled crab. Scrubs his skin until it stings. Slathers on some of the moisturiser his sister keeps buying him, an eco-friendly unscented soft cream not tested on animals and designed to make his face feel like a baby's bottom. He snickers at the thought. His sister means well, and he's grateful somewhere deep down in the sarcasm over it all. He's not bad-looking—well, apart from not having a single visible muscle anywhere. He's just…plain. A smattering of hair spreads across the base of his stomach, while his chest is smooth. Soft darkness covers his arms and legs. The stubble on his chin from today's shave is coarse against his hand as he massages in the cream.

His poor, neglected body hasn't seen the inside of a gym in years, and the lack of sunshine has made his summer skin turn pale and grey. He's not a catch, in any shape or form, but he gets away with it, using his charm and his mouth to his advantage. Girls like when you talk a load of crap. His friends just roll their eyes, as they've heard the pathetic inner monologue that kind of spews from his mouth when he can't control himself. He's a hapless idiot. A charmer. A pretender. *A liar.*

His bed is cold, and his mattress is lumpy. He sighs as he pulls his pyjama pants up his legs—last year's Christmas joke. The whole family were gifted themed pyjama sets and walked around like they were hosting some crazy fan convention all through January. He's lost the top, though, along with the hat that came with it.

The one flat pillow that lives on his bed feels damp against his skin as he folds it in half to make a decent wedge under his head, and he should really invest in a decent blanket. One of those soft fleecy ones he can wrap up in, the softness surrounding him like a warm hug. He needs to go shopping.

No, he doesn't. He needs to go down one flight of stairs and fall headfirst into the bed of clouds down there, full of warmth and smells and feathery pillows…and a man who won't know what's hit him if the deranged bloke from upstairs appears in his bed again.

Finally, Erik breaks. Because it's been three days. Three days of agonising over how to apologise. Turn it into some kind of joke? Make out it was a drunken mistake because he's an idiot? Except he doesn't want to apologise. He wants to do it again.

It's beyond foolish. It will be a total disaster, but Erik doesn't care anymore. He swings his legs out of bed before fear and rational thoughts can stop him, grabs his phone and keys, then slams the door shut on his way out.

Six

Oskar has two more episodes to go, and he has already decided that this is the worst series he has watched in a long time. Some British drama about a doctor who suspects her husband is having an affair, and she keeps looking at her iPhone, then drives for miles stalking him, when she could just look him up on 'Find my friends'. Oskar could've written a better script, thrown in a few twists and turns and pointed out that she's holding the medical equipment upside down as she yells at her colleague over missed test results.

It's awful, but he keeps watching. He might as well know how it ends so he can spend the rest of tomorrow at peace rather than agonising over some stupid TV drama.

Still, he feels a little better today, having eaten properly and drunk his two litres of water. He also limited himself to a thirty-minute run to give his knee a rest, not that his knee feels any better. It pounds and throbs under the duvet as he wriggles his hips to change position, then throws himself onto his side and lets the laptop bounce gently against the mattress.

He just can't get comfortable. Can't calm the uneasiness in his stomach.

The girls keep looking at him when he goes out there, to the common room. Carolina winks and laughs, and Freddie ogles as if Oskar's a random celebrity of some sorts. Like he's seeing him in a brand-new light.

And they all talk, no doubt about him. He can almost feel their eyes burning holes in the back of his neck when he walks by. The stares. The whispers. Well, at least Naomi was smiling out there at dinner, sitting cross-legged at the table, eating her vegetable stir-fry. She even let him do her hands again and promised she'd keep the thin, cotton, medical gloves on so the cream would have a chance to sink in. He needs to go buy some more ointment and gloves for her, for the next time. Because there *will* be a next time. There always is.

He supposes it was all meant to be, this becoming a doctor. He always loved puzzles as a child, and people are exactly that. Human puzzles that you have to twist and turn the pieces until you find where they fit. He gets Naomi and her mismatched little pieces. He understands how to put them back into place. He just can't figure out how to finish the puzzle. Find that missing piece. There must be a way to make her whole again. Just like there must be a way of healing himself.

Because Oskar is not whole, he thinks to himself when there is a soft knock on his door. He is not whole at all. If he was a proper, functioning human being, a knock on the door wouldn't set his heart into a chaotic pulse of terror. He wouldn't be sitting bolt upright in his bed, frozen to the bone in sheer panic.

The door opens and closes, and there he is. The dude from upstairs. Standing in the doorway and looking down at where Oskar is still sitting bolt upright in his bed.

"Hi," the dude says, and surprisingly, that makes Oskar a little calmer because he looks as terrified as Oskar feels.

"It's…like, almost midnight," Oskar blurts before he can engage his brain. "Are you all right?"

"Couldn't sleep," the guy says. *Erik says. His name is Erik.*

"Me neither." Oskar doesn't know where all these words are coming from. He doesn't talk this much. Especially to strangers who turn up in his room in the middle of the night.

Erik stays where he is, leaning against the wall. His hair is a damp mess on his head, like he has just showered. His hoodie is wrinkled, and he's wearing Christmas pyjama pants with Star Wars logos randomly mixed with Santa hats patterned over his legs.

"Also, my bed is nowhere near as comfortable as yours. I have total bed envy." Erik has this little twinkle in his eye that Oskar can't read, like he's teasing him but at the same time not. There is still that horrible fear in his eyes that makes Oskar go all soft inside. Makes him want to wrap Erik up in soft, padded, sterile bandages until he is all calm and safe again.

His head is a mess. Fact. There is no denying it. This will all end in disaster. Oskar almost laughs at the inevitability as he pats the pillow next to him, but, he reasons, what's the worst that could happen? The guy laughing in his face and hurling insults at him? It's not like they're friends. It's not like he has anything to lose.

"God, I love your bed." Erik laughs and pulls the hoodie over his head revealing a thin T-shirt underneath with a massive rip in the sleeve. Apparently, he's bad at this clothes thing too. Oskar couldn't dress himself if his life depended on it, which is why he wears stuff until it gets eaten by the industrial-sized washing machines in the laundry block or simply falls to pieces in his hands.

Erik throws his hoodie carelessly on the floor as he dives onto the bed and with no shame crawls under the duvet, puffs up the pillows under his head and flashes that smile, the one that births butterflies in Oskar's stomach and sets his cheeks on fire.

"Is this okay?" Erik asks. There is that fear again.

"Yeah, yeah, totally. Plenty of space," Oskar stutters and waves at the screen on his laptop, where the TV doctor is waving her phone about, looking distraught.

"What are you watching?" Erik is still finding his chill, pushing the pillows around and tugging at the duvet so he can bunch it up against his chest.

"Totally random BBC drama with all these loose strings that just don't add up. I don't know why I keep watching." Oskar slams the laptop shut and places it on the desk by the side of the bed.

"You should watch *The Fall*. I think it's on **NRK** online. Really clever drama from a few years back. Some serial killer. It's really good." Erik looks at him, then closes his eyes.

Oskar has the urge to reach out and sweep the hair from his face, stroke his freckled skin. Brush away the eyelash stuck to his eyelid. There's a little bit of moisture at the corner of his eye. A tiny teardrop that floods Oskar's head with ridiculous feelings again.

He doesn't do any of those things. Just crawls underneath the duvet and switches off his bedside lamp.

"Do you need an alarm?" he asks. Like it's totally normal. Like this isn't a freaky dream he'll wake up from in a minute. This doesn't happen in real life. People just don't come and sleep in other people's beds for no reason.

"Got it set on my phone, stashed in my boxers," Erik mumbles drowsily. Oskar can feel his breath on his face. They're a little too close for comfort.

"You shouldn't keep your phone so close to your body. The radiation could cause…"

He needs to stop talking. Stop asking stupid questions before this Erik has enough and gets up and walks out, never to come back. He should savour this. Remember it for the rest of his life.

"Yeah, I know. You sound like my mum." Erik shuffles, and the light from the phone momentarily brightens up the room before the space is plunged back into darkness.

"How did you get in? Wasn't the front door locked?" Oskar grimaces, grateful for the dark. Why is he still talking?

"Same key as for upstairs," Erik says. "And anyway, you should lock *your* door at night. You never know who might crawl in and sleep in your bed. Your bed is awesome. I might stay here forever."

There is laughter in Erik's voice, and Oskar matches it with a soft giggle, surprising himself.

"Yeah. I should, shouldn't I? You can stay. I don't mind."

Tension creeps up in his shoulders, and he turns over and finds that he is, yet again, balanced on the edge of the bed, as far away as possible from the man who has joined him. He doesn't mind. Truly. He doesn't mind at all. So why won't his brain shut down? Why can't he just stop thinking? Slow down the thoughts churning through his brain like cars on a racetrack.

"Night, Disney Prince."

"Night." Oskar's body is a mess. He turns onto his back and speaks again. "My name is Oskar."

"Hi, Oskar. I'm Erik."

"I know," he squeaks out.

"I knew too," Erik says softly. "Oskar Høiland, right?"

"Yeah."

"Night, night, Oskar Høiland."

"Night, night, Erik from Upstairs."

Erik chuckles, then sighs as he bunches the duvet into a ball in his arms, leaving Oskar half-uncovered. Not that he cares.

Astonishingly, Oskar sleeps, deep and dreamless, until the metallic shrill of his phone echoes through the darkness and it's morning again.

SEVEN

He stretches and pushes his palms against the wall over his head. Pushes and stretches until every muscle in his body is singing with that slight hint of pain, his toes pointing towards the opposite wall, his feet hanging over the edge of the bed.

His bed. Which is cold and empty again as he reaches out and punches the shrilling phone next to him. Punches it again. With his fist.

Fuck.

He's not here. Gone again like some imaginary shadow in the night. Oskar curls into himself and groans in frustration.

In a way, it's good. No more awkward conversation. No worries about who does what. In any case, he has a lecture in two hours and needs to prep the immunology case study beforehand, so he's ready for the group lab session afterwards. He also needs to run.

Well, no, he doesn't need to run. Nobody *needs* to run. But his days always seem to flow better after he has exhausted himself.

Sitting up, he piles the pillows behind his back and flips his laptop open. Types a few sentences aimlessly to open his argument.

He has no argument. He doesn't know shit about immunology right now. Not a clue.

"Morning, sleepyhead."

That's his door. Slamming shut. And there is Erik.

Erik. And Oskar can't help himself. He bursts into laughter. Erik is wearing Oskar's smelly old dressing gown and Carolina's unicorn slippers, as he sits himself down on the bed in front of Oskar, feet dangling over the side, and hands him a cup of coffee.

"My feet were cold, okay?" Erik smirks looking a little embarrassed. "So Carolina lent me these. She's hilarious."

"No Disney nickname for her?" He tries not to smile. Tries desperately not to smile.

"Nah. She's far too cool for a nickname. She's Girl Caro. As opposed to Boy Carlos who lives with us upstairs."

"What about the rest of us?" Oskar takes a sip of his coffee, letting the warm liquid coat his throat as Erik leans in and steals the cup back and takes a long sip from the other side. Oskar raises an eyebrow. Erik raises one back as if to say, "So what? We share a bed. We can quite happily share a cup. Like normal people."

But there is nothing normal about this. Nothing at all.

"Oh, we have the Ice Princess, who treats everyone to the ice-cold stare, even though Victor upstairs has the biggest crush on her. He is, like, obsessed to the point that it's embarrassing. He writes poetry about raven-haired girls with red, pouting lips. Someone needs to slap him. Or pretty much get him laid. Then there is Camp Rock."

"Camp Rock?" Oskar almost splutters on a gulp of coffee before Erik rescues the cup.

"His name's Freddie, I think. Fourth-year psychology dude? Camp as fuck but solid as a rock. He got Mikael out of a serious situation last year, and Adam says if we ever say a bad word about him, we'll meet his fist down a dark alley. You don't mess with Adam. So, Camp Rock. Yup. We suck at these nicknames, don't we?"

Oskar nods, mesmerised by Erik, who wriggles his feet again, and Oskar steals the coffee cup for another sip before catching his breath.

Erik is still going on, because apparently coffee makes him talkative.

"Then you have the Fake Bake girls, Ingrid and Madeleine. Brown like gingerbread men in the middle of winter, caked in make-up, and everything that comes out of their mouths is mind-blowingly dull. Like reality-shows-and-beauty-treatments kind of dull. And, by the way, I think Madeleine has a crush on you. She was seconds away from stabbing me with the bread knife out there and obviously hates my guts."

"Bullshit," Oskar says. He goes to take another sip of coffee from the now empty cup and no doubt looks like an idiot as Erik hands him the bowl that has been sat in his other hand the whole time. Shifting slightly, he fishes a spoon from the dressing-gown pocket and hands it to Oskar with a triumphant grin. Seeing as he's already practically lying in Oskar's lap, he easily grabs a book from the desk and starts to flick through it, though he's not looking at the pages.

"Ingrid and Maddie aren't always dull," Oskar says on their behalf. "Ingrid is majoring in remote medicine, which is really amazingly useful. She's going off to work for Médecins Sans Frontières in the fall and has all these…you know…ideals and goals."

He can't even put together a coherent sentence when Erik is staring at him.

"Cool," Erik says and pretends to read something in the book. Then he drops it onto the bed and smiles at Oskar again. Like, charming-smiles at him. Like he actually likes him.

"Madeleine is studying human rights law." Oskar doesn't know what else to do but keep talking. "She runs the University Amnesty branch and is really involved, you know, does their social media and stuff, and you know…she can be nice, and…anyway, she's not dull."

He should at least shut up long enough to engage his brain so he can speak in grammatically correct, full sentences.

"I asked the girls out there to help me make breakfast for you. They said you only eat birdseed with that oat milk stuff, and no sugar. Madeleine said you're some kind of health nut and don't eat anything with sugar in it. That's crazy, by the way. I need to introduce you to the Dutch Lotus spread Ammar buys. You have it on toast, and it's heavenly. Have you tried those new instant gingerbread latte mixes? They're like crack. Once you start, you can't stop."

"Sounds weird. Honestly? Gingerbread coffee?" Oskar wrinkles his nose, and Erik laughs at him. Oskar's stomach has gone all warm again because Erik is being so cute, it's making Oskar's teeth hurt a little, along with his cheeks. Mostly because he can't seem to stop smiling.

"Do you like to read? Stuff like this?" Erik is back to flicking aimlessly through the book. Some random poetry collection, full of broken people and jet-black hearts.

"Sometimes." Oskar relaxes back against the pillows, awkwardly scooping soggy muesli into his mouth. "Reading other people's thoughts sometimes makes me feel normal, like my life isn't as shit and hopeless as I think it is."

"What's wrong with your life? You're acing it through medical school. I mean, Hassan upstairs is in your year. He says you take really good notes, which you let people borrow, then you go pass every exam like it's easy. You live in the coolest dorm on campus, with all the fun people, and…look at you. You could have anyone you wanted. You only have to smile, and people…"

Erik suddenly goes quiet and looks worried again, as if he's said too much, crossed a line, and doesn't want Oskar to be angry at him. Like he doesn't want to upset Oskar, full stop.

"They all think we're shagging," Oskar blurts out, his voice low and gruff. "That we have some kind of thing going on."

"Is that bad? I'm sorry if I've embarrassed you. I didn't think. I…I just wanted to bring you breakfast before I left. To say thank you. For letting me sleep with you again." Erik sits up, his hair all over the place, still with that terrified look back on his face.

"You didn't sleep with me…" Oskar starts, then groans in frustration. "Fuck, my life is going to be hell now. They don't let things slide in this dorm. Everything gets fucking blown out of proportion."

Erik sits there looking at his hands. His shoulders hunched as he starts to remove the dressing gown.

"I should go," he says. "Sorry I made things worse. I didn't mean to."

"Don't go. Sorry." Oskar is panicking. *Please don't leave. Please stay and talk to me. Make me feel like I'm okay and this is fine. Because this is the most fine I have felt for a long time. Even though I am totally fucked.* "I don't know what I'm doing, Erik. I've never had a…never been with anyone. Fuck, I've never even been kissed. That's how much of a loser I am? And I don't know how to deal with people thinking I'm something I'm not. I'm nothing. Nobody. I don't know what I am doing…" He trails off as Erik's hand lands on his shoulder, strong and supporting.

"That doesn't matter." His voice is low and kind. "What the fuck does it matter, Oskar? But if it's important to you, I'll help you. We can get you both kissed and laid if that is what you want. Just tell me who you're crushing on, and we can kind of launch a plan. I mean, I owe you a favour. Hell, I owe you two favours. You let me sleep here twice…next to you, not with you. Okay?" His strong fingers lightly massage Oskar's shoulders. Erik takes a deep breath and continues. "You need to keep track so you can cash in on all these things I need to help you with, to make this up to you."

"You don't owe me anything," Oskar whispers. He can't even begin to feel embarrassed anymore. This is so way-beyond embarrassing it's just plain awful. Awkward and stupid.

"Three favours. One more for embarrassing you in front of your friends out there. So let me know what you want, and I will make it happen. Promise. I'm a damn good wingman. Just ask Ammar and Mathias upstairs. I pretty much am responsible for Mathias losing his virginity a few months back. Pushed him onto this girl, and hey presto! They're still together. I did good." Erik winks and shakes Oskar's shoulder, his grip still firm, burning through his thin T-shirt and then into his cheek.

"Chin up, Disney Prince. We'll get you kissed and laid in no time. Deal?"

Oskar nods like a fool, and Erik winks again, then gets up and wraps Oskar's dressing gown tighter around his shoulders, picks up his hoodie off the floor, and does a stupid salute.

"See you around, Disney Prince." Then he leaves, closing the door softly behind him.

❅

Erik doesn't cry until he is safely in his room upstairs, naked in the shower with the far-too-hot water running over his body. He cries for being stupid. For being reckless and unkind.

He cries because he is about to lose the one thing he really wants. He wants Oskar, and that is a terrifying thing to admit to himself. Oskar, who is beautiful and kind and frightened and embarrassed and…and now Erik has promised to help him get kissed. Get laid. Help him find someone else. Because Oskar obviously doesn't want Erik. He's made that pretty clear, the anger and embarrassment radiating from his body like poisonous vapour in some fucked-up sci-fi movie.

He should get going if he's going to make Graphics Lab before nine. Instead, he curls up around Oskar's dressing gown and buries his nose in the scent of the man downstairs, the man with the terrified eyes and the sadness and all those stupid worries in his tensed-up shoulders.

Erik wants to kiss them away. Hold him and shush him and tell him that it doesn't matter. Nothing bloody matters anymore. Because right now, he feels, and for once he lets himself revel in it, however much it hurts.

In a way, he supposes it's karma hitting him right in the face. Every unkind word Erik has ever thrown out in anger is coming back at him. Every stupid joke and stunt he has pulled, things that were funny at the time but now he cringes at the crap he used to churn out to make people laugh. But it was never about making people laugh. It was something to hide behind. Lies. So many fucking lies.

He's hurt people. He's made his friends feel small, made other people feel worthless so he could feel better. He's not a good person, he never was. And now he's lying here like the stupid piece of shit he is. What was he thinking? That this would turn into some kind of fairy tale where he would skip off into the sunset with his Disney Prince?

He deserves this. All of this. He's brought it on himself.

He feels…and it's fucking painful.

EIGHT

Oskar is grateful for a lot of things, but right now, he is just amazingly grateful for the Christmas holidays or Festive Season or whatever it is politically correct to call it these days. Christmas means everyone goes home, the dorm falls quiet, and people leave him the fuck alone.

Because the taunts haven't stopped. They don't intend to be mean or bully him or anything, but he can hear it in their voices. The little digs. Asking questions. The looks and winks. Even Freddie, who usually has Oskar's back, can't stop smiling at him like he knows all Oskar's secrets.

He knows fuck all. Just like Oskar.

Naomi gives him a hug as she walks out the door, her backpack slung over her shoulder and her hat pulled almost over her eyes.

"Thank you," she whispers in his ear. "Thank you for being everything I need right now. You're a good friend, Oskar. The best." She taps her pocket where he has stuck the bag from the pharmacy, which contains a new tube of cream that's a little stronger and thicker than the usual stuff, as he knows she'll struggle over the next couple of days. She's going back to the scene of the crime. Back to her parents who don't understand. Back to her friends who expect her to be someone she hasn't been for years. It's hard. Oskar knows. He knows because he doesn't go back at all.

"Merry Christmas, Princess," he whispers back, pleased with his choice of endearment. She might look like an ice princess, but there is nothing cold about Naomi. She feels too much, loves too hard and breaks too easily. "Be strong. Breathe. Look after your hands. And call me if you need me."

"I will." She smiles as she walks out the door. "Merry Christmas."

The dorm is quiet, which is the way Oskar needs it to be as he curls up in bed. It's been almost five days now. Five long days since Erik walked out of his room and out of his life, and Oskar has finally changed his sheets. Washed the scent and the memories and the fucked-up daydreams right out of his bed in time for Christmas.

The yellow glow of the electric candle arch on the windowsill washes over the cheap paper star he picked up at the Co-op, along with his milk and sausages and a pack of meatballs. He should have bought some wine, maybe a bottle of gløgg, but he couldn't be bothered to join the outrageous queues at the Alcohol shop, along with the rest of Oslo shopping for their parties and festive treats.

The Christmas star was a mistake because you need a nail to hang it on, and Oskar has neither a nail nor a hammer, so the pathetic-looking paper star lies on its side looking sad and miserable despite its sparkly glory. Typical him. He should left it in the Co-op, accepted the fact that he is no good at any kind of interior design. Unlike his mum, who used to dress the house up like a show home, matching baubles and stars on the perfectly shaped fake tree and a designer wreath from the posh florist in town hanging on their door.

He hasn't even got a candle to light. No Christmas cheer here. Not that Oskar has anything to cheer about. His life is slowly going back to normal, and hopefully, when people return in the New Year, everything will be forgotten. New dramas and gossip and rumours that Oskar was shagging someone will be yesterday's news. Done and dusted.

Then, suddenly, there is the slam of the front door, followed by the clunk of the handle on his room door as it opens and closes with a bang.

"Hi."

Oskar has thought about this. He has planned in his head how he will tell Erik to leave him alone and find someone else to pester. Hell, he could even offer a good discount on a bed and bedding if it would keep Erik away from him. But he doesn't say any of that. He just sits in his bed with a piece of pizza dangling out of his mouth, staring at Erik like he is some apparition of Jesus Christ himself on the night before Christmas.

As if he belongs there, Erik throws himself down on Oskar's bed and shuffles the pillows under his head. On *his* side of the bed, Oskar thinks, like Erik now has his own side of Oskar's bed. Like this is a thing.

"Hi?" he stutters out. The pizza in his mouth tastes like cardboard.

"You still here? Not heading home for Christmas?"

"Nope." Oskar tries to sound cheerful. Indifferent.

"Why the hell not? Where are your parents?"

"Mindfulness retreat somewhere in Sweden. They go every year. Then they come back all zen and chill for the New Year and get shitfaced-drunk with all their friends. Beats me why they do it, but it's not my kind of thing. They did offer." Oskar hasn't said so many words in one go for days, and he has to catch his breath before continuing. "So, I'm staying here. I'm finally going to watch that *Stranger Things* thing on Netflix and work on my genealogy paper. I'm a loser, Erik. Get used to it."

He doesn't mean to sound snarky, but it's been five days, and he's a little pissed off, though he doesn't fully understand why. He doesn't understand shit. But, hey. What's new?

"Sorry," Erik says. Just like that.

"Sorry for what?" Oskar turns to face him, which is when he notices Erik is a mess. He looks like he's been crying, and Oskar's stomach knots into a ball of angst. He should have noticed the second Erik walked into the room.

"For messing shit up. I just can't help it, it seems."

"You haven't messed anything up. Chill. It's Christmas. Are you going home?" *Don't get too deep. Don't ask. Don't make this messier than it is. Just let this slide. Let him just...* He doesn't know what he is on about in his head anymore. His brain stops functioning when Erik turns up, like he totally loses control of himself. "Pizza?" he offers, holding out the plate where a single, cold piece of plastic-cheese-covered cardboard lingers.

"No, thanks," Erik mutters and shuffles nervously, jiggling his legs to get comfortable, his breath strained. "I still owe you a load of favours, and here I am like some jerk, needing to ask you for some more."

Erik has been agonising for days, camping out in his bed in Oskar's dressing gown that now doesn't smell anything like Oskar. It smells of Erik's sweat and stale milk from when he spilled his latte over himself crying into his phone while his mum tried to send virtual hugs to him over the airways. He needs to give the dressing gown back. Except his plan was to wash it and then sneak down here in the middle of the night and rub it all over Oskar, so he could steal it back and sleep with it at night.

Well, that genius idea didn't work because the laundry room was fully booked all weekend.

So here he is. Going all out for the real thing instead, like the idiot he is, heading headfirst into a guaranteed shitstorm of a disaster as he pulls out his mum's genius plan B.

"Shoot. What do you need?" Oskar smiles and shrugs his shoulders like Erik is completely normal. *No problem, mate. I can do you a favour. It's fine.*

Except nothing is fine.

"Can I stay with you tonight? Please? I'll sneak out before anyone sees me in the morning. I just need to sleep, and I sleep better with you. In your bed. I love your bed."

"You have a fucked-up relationship with my bed." Oskar laughs. "That's a joke, by the way."

Erik pushes away the thought of what he really wants to say. "Yeah. I have a thing for your bed." He rubs his eyes, wipes his mouth with the back of his hand and sinks down under the covers. "Please can I stay?"

"Of course! Always." Oskar sighs, his voice resigned as if disappointed with his lack of willpower. He probably wants to tell Erik to fuck off. To grow the fuck up and stop messing around.

"That's four favours I owe you now. Probably five after I ask the other thing I was going to ask."

"Should I be worried?" Oskar sounds cool and calm and even manages another smile, but his hands are gripping mindlessly at the sheets.

Erik doesn't usually speak to people like this, but Oskar does something to him. Makes him lose all his inhibitions because he doesn't judge Erik by all the crap that comes out of his mouth. He just smiles at him, as if what he says is the most adorable shit ever.

"I want you to come home with me for Christmas. It will be fun. Just my mum and dad and Uncle Asbjørn and my sisters and their kids. It's pretty boring, but there's always loads of food, and we play all these board games and watch Christmas specials on Eurosport. It's safe. Easy. Chill. I never bring anyone with me, but it would be nice to have the company, someone I can hang out with instead of just building Lego and playing The Amazing Labyrinth until I pass out from caffeine withdrawal. My parents don't drink anything containing caffeine. It's pretty painful."

He holds his breath, while his heart is beating so fast he thinks he might faint. All the blood is rushing to his head in a thunderous silence while Oskar lies there, obviously stunned to silence by Erik's frankly idiotic request. It's a brilliant idea, even his mum said so. Well, it was her idea. Her stupid, stupid idea, and now Erik wants to hide under the covers and never see the light of day again. Ever. Death is an option. Just kill him. Now. *Please.*

"Really?" Oskar says, and then he falls quiet.

❄

This is the part where Oskar says *thanks, but no thanks* and keeps his anxieties in check while carefully calculating how much his body can take. The part where his brain jumps to life and finds imaginary hurdles giving him every excuse to say no. He doesn't do parties. He doesn't do strangers. He especially doesn't do Erik Nøst Hansen and his family and Christmas and all that. He just…doesn't.

"Okay?" Oskar's mouth says, while his brain screams like there is full-blown murder going on in his head and his hands shake, and Erik's face lights up like Oskar has offered him the moon and the stars.

"Bring your running gear. We have this amazing track in the forest at the back of the garden. Five K of snow-covered ski tracks, but there's a good walking track alongside it where people run and walk. It's pretty well trodden at Christmas, so you can get a nice run in. It will be great. Thank you."

"Okay?" Oskar says again, his mouth dry and his brain scrambling. He reaches out and switches off the light so he can hide in the safety of darkness as Erik fidgets with his phone and the duvet again. His feet nudge Oskar's, making him jump.

"Sorry," Erik whispers. "Just trying to plug my phone in. Do you mind?"

"Go to sleep," Oskar whispers back.

"We need to leave at four tomorrow evening. Does that work? I have some stuff to do in the morning, and there's a train at five, which brings us home in time for dinner."

"Mm-hmm," Oskar mumbles because right now, he has lost all ability to speak, let alone form coherent thoughts. He needs to get up and brush his teeth. Lock his door. Bang his head against the wall in agony over his own stupidity.

"Okay," Erik says. "Sleep well, my Disney Prince."

Oskar swallows the laughter that brews in his throat. He is no one's fucking Disney Prince. He is nobody. He's nothing.

He reaches out and clumsily pats Erik's shoulder. A little pat. Warm skin under the palm of his hand.

"Night, night, Erik from Upstairs," he whispers.

There is no reply. Only the soft breaths of the man next to him in his bed.

NINE

23rd December

He's true to his word, Oskar thinks to himself as he wakes up, lying diagonally across the bed with his feet sticking out over the edge and the duvet wrapped around his waist like some oversized nappy. Looking like a complete dork, no doubt.

The sheets are empty and cold, and he can't decide if that's good or bad, sad or plain pathetic. No. It's good. Simple. Safe. Yet he has an ache in his chest, like something is missing. Ridiculous, he knows that. Erik is just this lonely, weird-ass dude Oskar needs to figure out how to ditch before he gets pulled into something he can't control. This is not a healthy friendship or the start of a beautiful business opportunity. They are not colleagues or teammates, and Erik has nothing to win from sharing space or oxygen with Oskar. *Fuck!* Even being in Oskar's vicinity has no gains for Erik. He just doesn't get it. Why him? Why the hell him?

Rather than lying in bed going over it again and again, Oskar runs for an hour while his knees scream and his thoughts align in neat, little rows as he likes them. He can do this. He can survive this Christmas thing. It will be what? A day and a bit? He can always fake an emergency and get the hell out of there. It can't be that bad. It will be fine.

At least the dorm is deserted as he moves his laptop out into the common room and forces himself write a few pages of genealogy—developing research, facts and figures. The ease of studying takes over, and he zones out of the real world and lets his brain do all the work while the facts dance on the screen in front of him. It's easy. Controlled. Making perfect sense.

Not like Erik, who is random and a little bit weird. Why the hell is he hassling Oskar? What the hell does he want?

He tries to shrug off those thoughts and get his brain back into gear. Get this paper finished, because he's almost there. He is so fucking close. Just a few more pages.

He gets nothing done. By three thirty, he is pacing the common room, fully dressed with his knitted hat pulled over his head, the scarf around his neck strangling him in the heat inside. He's packed a bag and had a full-blown panic attack because he has nothing to give Erik's parents. Not even a lousy box of chocolates. He can only hope he'll have time to grab something random and impersonal at the station, then pretend he has actually thought about it.

His mother hates those kinds of gifts. She buys thoughtful, personalized presents for people. Handmade crafts with bespoke touches, embroidered names in rustic stitching on organically dyed fabric that she wraps in colour-coordinated tissue paper with proper fabric bows. She would die from shame if she knew he was even contemplating buying a box of cheap chocolates from the newsagents at Oslo Central station.

But it's not like Oskar has a choice. Nothing is open late on 23rd December. Normal people are home preparing for Christmas Eve, cooking and wrapping and being all festive with their friends and families. Meanwhile, Oskar is hyperventilating and sweating like it's a hot summer's day and he's stuck in a sauna wearing his winter jacket.

By four o'clock, he gives up and goes outside. There's no movement upstairs, no slamming of doors. No loud footfalls in the stairwell. Rounding the front of the building, his boots leave virgin tracks in the new snow. Soft flakes falling silently through the dark winter air.

He stands there for a moment, just taking it all in. The random patterns created by the enormous flakes. The silence. In the orange glow of the streetlights, the world seems slightly magical, steeped in some spell that makes everything seem soft and quiet.

"It's amazing if you lie down and look up. It's like looking into eternity. Just flakes appearing out of nowhere, hurtling down towards Earth. Come. Come lie down with me."

In this Bed of Snowflakes We Lie

Oskar has always suspected Erik is a bit strange—that he does all these random things normal people wouldn't dream of doing.

Like throwing your bags on the ground and lying flat on your back in the snow so you can stare up at the dark sky.

"Come on. Lie down with me," Erik urges, patting the snow next to him with his gloved hand.

And Oskar does it. Because why the hell not? It's not like anyone is watching, and he is resigning himself to the fact that somehow, Erik can get him to do weird things too. But he doesn't lie down. He sits on the ground, stretching out his legs and kicking his feet awkwardly in the snow.

It's freezing, his bum already aching from the cold wetness seeping through his jeans. He should have worn long johns, like normal people do when the temperature drops below -15°C. He knows how to dress in winter—layers and waterproofs and thermal underwear—but he gets too hot inside and too cold outside, and he…

He needs to stop thinking so much.

Erik waves his arms backwards and forwards in the snow and recites theatrically, "In this bed of snowflakes we lie. The soft cool bedding that falls from the sky."

"Is that a real poem?" Oskar laughs self-consciously. Erik is right, though. Looking up at the snowflakes hurtling towards you is quite cool. Totally zen, almost mesmerising. Even though his bum is very, very cold and wet.

"Nah. Just made it up to impress you. Proper posh shit—taking you out in the snow to read poetry to you." Erik laughs. "But, seriously, Oskar, I read something once, about snowflakes being nature's most fragile creation, but look what they can do when you squash them together."

He picks up handfuls of snow, pressing them between his palms to form a ball. "Hard as ice. Tough as anything. Just like people. Never underestimate people, Oskar. We may be weak on our own, but together, with the right person… Well, nothing can touch us. Love does that to people. You find your person, and they make you strong. Happy. Light. Invincible. Like you're floating on air. Do you know what I mean?" Erik looks at him, his face full of honesty. Of questions. Of kindness. All those things that make Oskar feel a little strange, and he can't stop looking back. Can't form a single, coherent thought in his head. Erik is ridiculous, lying there in the snow and talking about love like he knows all the secrets of the universe.

Finally, Oskar's brain reconnects, and he realises he can no longer feel his buttocks. "We need to get going. When did you say the train was?" He's also getting a little bit uncomfortable lying here with Erik staring at him.

"Shit. Forgot. We'd better move. Come on, Disney Prince." Erik scrambles to his feet and reaches out his hand to grab Oskar's, pulling him up from the snow leaving two pretty random snow angels behind.

"I forgot to make wings." Oskar laughs and points at the outline of his arms, which make his snow angel look like a stick insect, while Erik's has magnificent wings.

"You're perfect as you are," Erik says and wraps his glove-clad hands around Oskar's face. Then he kind of freezes up and blinks before his face opens into a shy smile. "Promise me one thing."

Erik's gloves are cold against Oskar's cheeks, and he's giving him that look again—the one that makes Oskar's stomach clench with nerves and makes his hands shake yet calms the storms raging in his chest. Luckily, Erik takes his silence as permission to continue.

"Promise me that this Christmas, you are just you. Don't pretend to be something you're not. Because it's exhausting, believe me. I know what it's like. I spend most of my life pretending to be this person so far removed from who I really am, and it drains your soul. My mum would say it rots your heart. She's strange. You will love her. Anyway. Just be you, Oskar. Everyone will love you just as you are. So, no pretending, no trying to be polite and perfect and all that. Just chill with me. Hang out and do Christmas. With me. Being me. Okay?"

Oskar nods, like he knows what he's agreeing to when in reality he hasn't got a clue what Erik is on about. How can he be anything but himself? He is who he is. He's a mess. A nerd. A nervous, insecure man with nothing to offer the world except an almost half-completed medical degree.

"I know what you're thinking," Erik says. "Switch off all the thoughts. You get all these little lines on your forehead when you're worried and anxious—when you think I'm pulling a fast one on you. I'm not. I like you and I want to hang out with you. I just hope you want to hang out with me too, and that you'll still speak to me in two days' time after surviving the Nøst Hansen family Christmas."

He winks and pulls Oskar in for a hug, wraps his arms tightly around him in the middle of the street. Outside Dorm 212, where the snow falls around them, and the muffled sound of a car starting up is the only thing piercing the silence.

So, Oskar gives in. For once, he doesn't give a fuck. He hugs Erik back, pressing his face into Erik's scarf as Erik's breaths puff, steady and strong, against his cheek.

They stand there for what feels like hours. It's probably no more than a minute. But Oskar doesn't want to let go, not when he has all this newfound tactility. He likes that Erik touches him. He likes Erik's hands on his face. He likes the feel of Erik's body against his, his own gloved hands on someone else's clothes.

He almost whines when Erik pulls away, takes his phone out of his pocket, and checks the time.

"We need to go, Disney Prince. Let's go do Christmas."

Picking up his backpack from the ground, Erik wrangles it awkwardly over his thick jacket, grabs the large shopping bag next to it, which is bursting with neatly wrapped parcels, and does a little twirl in the snow. Oskar rolls his eyes.

"I haven't got anything for your parents," he says, as they set off for the town, and Erik laughs reassuringly, reaching out to touch Oskar's arm.

"I bought them something from both of us. It's fine. Just relax. Don't stress about anything. Okay?"

For the first time, Oskar smiles for real and nudges Erik's arm with his shoulder as they cross the road. Erik nudges him back—a reminder that they're good.

And Oskar thinks this might just be okay. Two days. Two nights.

It will be okay. It has to be.

TEN

What Erik should have done was plan. Booked one of those 'comfort tickets' with reserved seats ahead of time using his nifty student card for a good discount, and then he should have perhaps asked his parents to pick them up from the station instead of having to hang around for the bus. Because, of course, when you rock up on 23rd December, along with the rest of Norway trying to get to Moss, you're not going to get anywhere in comfort.

Moss. The godforsaken coastal town that Erik calls home. He used to hate it—the small-town gossip and suburban blandness of the street where he grew up. Now he kind of likes it in an almost grown-up way.

So, instead of being the perfect gentleman offering his Disney Prince a cup of coffee in the warmth of a padded seat en route to his humble palace, they find themselves squashed up by the door, sharing the slushy-wet floor space with a pram, a tiny yapping dog and about ten random people. Well, at least they got on, and they'll be home for dinner. Erik sighs and leans into Oskar, pressing in on him a little to check he's not freaking out. He's quiet, fiddling with the gloves in his hands.

"You okay?" Erik asks quietly.

"Yeah." Oskar smiles, but it's one of those nervous smiles. He's shit scared, and Erik doesn't blame him. Fuck, if this was Erik being dragged home to Oskar's parents for Christmas, he'd be locked in the on-board toilet by now, dry-retching into the steel sink and praying for a divine miracle.

But Oskar is brave. He's the bravest person Erik has ever met. He's nothing like Erik, who hides and dodges bullets left, right and centre, pretending when he should be real. At least he has his family, and his family is bloody awesome.

"My parents are kind of overgrown hippies." He thinks if he

can keep talking, churning out verbal diarrhoea for an hour, then neither of them will have to think about what they are actually doing. "They're both a little weird and wacky. Dad is a schoolteacher. He spends his days singing ABC songs and crawling around on his hands and knees with his pupils. The kids adore him. I wasn't allowed to be in his class when I started school, so I had this teacher called Tordis, who was about a hundred years old. She used to make us sit there in silence, doing our letters and numbers, when all we could hear were the kids in Dad's class, screaming and running and laughing. It felt like a punishment. Everyone wanted to be in my dad's class."

Erik has to take a deep breath while the train carriage shakes with the speed through a curve. He's talking too fast and tries to slow down.

"Mum owns this craft shop downtown, full of local gifts and souvenirs for the tourists. She also runs the Christmas market and is heavily into healing and alternative therapies. She's all about spreading love and kisses and hugging strangers and trees and all sorts. She'll hug you to death and insist you call her Mum. Just tell her to back off if it becomes too much. Or wink at me and I'll go put her on time out in the corner."

Erik lets a little laugh escape, and Oskar wipes his nose with the back of his hand—another nervous little twitch, Erik has noticed.

"You're okay," he whispers and leans closer, letting their heads touch for a while. Just catching his breath.

Oskar will be fine. It's Erik who might break. He's falling a little bit more in love with this bizarre human every day. Every hour.

Every minute he spends with Oskar makes his stomach twist in agony. There are so many things that can go wrong this Christmas. So many innocent words that will spill out of people's mouths and give him away.

One little word, and it will be game over.

If Erik lays his cards on the table and Oskar runs in fear, or even worse says those words that Erik fears the most—the rejection, the excuses…the very sensible excuses…

Of course, Oskar has every right to say, "Hey, I just don't feel that way about you." Because in all probability, Oskar is straight. Erik knows the odds are stacked against him. It would be just his luck that for the first time ever, his heart is all in, his whole body shivering in excitement, mixed with a healthy spoonful of terrifying fear, at the thought of being brave enough to steal a quick kiss from those lips…only to be rejected.

"Almost home," he says, trying to sound cheerful and happy, as Oskar rubs his nose again and offers him another tense little smile. "Fifteen more minutes."

Maybe half an hour more alone with Oskar. He'll just have to make the most of it.

They walk through the station, spilling out into the quiet street with a few slow passing cars, their tyres crackling against the hard snow. Erik has travelled this route more times than he cares to remember, and his head clogs with memories and scenes from his misspent youth. He rumbled around here with kids he used to know. People who once meant something to him, whom he now struggles to even remember.

"The first time I got drunk, I threw up behind the bench over there." He points and blushes in shame. *Way to go, Erik*. He's trying and failing to show off the quaint coastal town in the hope that Oskar will fall in love with it and maybe want to come back.

"You should see this place in summer when it's full of tourists—we need to go to Alby and buy you an Alby Kringle. It's the kind of thing people have on their bucket lists. They are just that good. And the beaches are amazing. We could have a barbecue on the rocks and just sit there and chill until we get cold, and then pitch a tent and sleep next to the water. I used to love that."

"I've never slept in a tent." Oskar chuckles nervously. "My parents aren't the camping type."

Erik lets his arm nudge Oskar's again. He needs to know he can—that Oskar is still his friend, whatever happens. *Please God, let Oskar still be my friend tomorrow.* "What are your parents like?"

"Dad is the CEO for Nordic Beds, Norway division, and Mum is a Neurosurgeon."

"No shit!" Erik's mouth falls wide open. "Seriously?"

Oskar nods. "So, no pressure on me, then. I want to go into paediatrics, I think. Maybe dermatology. Haven't quite studied enough to figure it all out. But then, if it all goes to shit, I can always flog beds. I would probably be good at that."

"And here is our bus," Erik declares, curling into a silly bow and waving his arm ahead of Oskar as the bus makes its slow turn into the bay. "I wish I could've arranged more appropriate transport for you, but Your Royal Highness will just have to make do with the number-twenty bus like the rest of us commoners."

"Shut up," Oskar hisses, but his face is flushed, and his eyes are crinkling at the corners, which makes Erik smile.

"You *will* go to the ball!" Erik announces. "You must, I insist!"

He's having fun. He thinks Oskar is too, despite constantly hiding his face inside his jacket collar and mostly nodding instead of speaking.

Erik taps his card over the ticket reader. He taps it twice. Honest, that's him. He's paying for two like a grown-up. They get seats next to each other and their thighs press gently together, which makes him all warm inside his heavy jacket.

The bus crosses over the canal, leaving the mainland for the island; Erik points out the small beach, the place he learned to swim, and the now quiet main street where he saw his first movie at the now long-gone cinema. "These flats are all new," he mumbles, not really knowing why. It's strange being back. It always is. This is home, yet he no longer belongs here.

Oskar nods politely, even though Erik can tell he is lost in his own head, staring absentmindedly into the steamed-up bus window while his hands fidget nervously with his gloves.

Erik holds onto Oskar's arm as they step off the bus, memorising the feel of his jacket and the way his breath forms clouds in the crisp air before the bus's departure leaves them in total darkness.

"It never gets this dark in Oslo," Oskar says quietly. "Too many lights in the city, I suppose."

"It's dark out here in the sticks. I used to carry a torch when I came home late at night, before they put up the streetlights in our road. Sometimes I couldn't see shit."

"Life before mobile phones," Oskar notes dryly, bringing his mobile up to shine light on the ground before promptly losing his footing and slipping on the sheet ice.

Erik's laughter echoes between the houses on the little road leading up towards a wooded area. Small, neat flakes fall around them as they walk. The houses are all lit up, stars and candles in the windows, open-flamed candle pots sitting in the snow along the road. A headless snowman graces the area where the road turns into a small track into the forest.

"The cross-country ski track starts here. It's about four-point-five K until you pop back out at the top of the clearing up there, where that streetlight is." Erik points, and Oskar cranes his neck to see. "And the red building over there is Hoppern School, where I went to school and my dad teaches. And here we are. Home sweet home. Welcome to Villa Nøst Hansen."

※

It's nothing special, Oskar thinks. Just a standard wooden free-standing house like all the others in the road, with snow piled deep around the Volvo parked in the driveway. But there are candles in every window and red showy curtains and lit paper stars and candle arches everywhere. The house screams Christmas. Family. All the things Oskar's house is missing.

His parents' neat house screams *Look at us! We're pretty goddamn perfect!* when they're not really. His dad works too much, his mum is a bossy pedant half the time, only to descend into a neurotic mess after a glass of wine, always worried about what her friends think and say and do, and Oskar. Well, there is no hope for Oskar.

※

"There'll be no peace and quiet from now on, but I promise they're all good people. Well, Uncle Asbjørn will ask you all kinds of questions, and my sister Emmy will interrogate you like a pro, but…"

Oskar's eyes are once again wide with fear, and Erik quietens.

He doesn't mean to do this. He knows he is overwhelming at the best of times, but God, he wants Oskar to have fun. To be loved. To feel what Erik feels whenever he is home, like he's cuddled up in this warm, fleecy blanket of love, where nothing in the world can hurt him. Apart from Lego bricks on the stairs and his dad's over-spicy mulled wine.

But Oskar clearly isn't feeling it, so Erik does the only thing he can think to do. He wraps Oskar in a hug. Scoops him up and buries his face in Oskar's scarf. It smells of soap and awesome beds and warm duvets and pillows that feel like clouds against your skin.

"If it all gets too much, just tap me on the arm. One tap means *help me, I'm struggling*. Two taps mean *get me out of here now*. Three taps? That's full red alert, and I promise I will get you out of the house and have you back in your own bed within the hour. Whatever the cost. Okay?"

"Erik, I'm not a child." Oskar sounds a little annoyed.

"I know. But…I don't know. I just don't want you to worry."

"I'm not worried." There are so many little frown lines on Oskar's face. His shoulders are practically up by his ears, and his jaw is locked. He is terrified, as Erik would be.

"Come on. Let's get this over with so we can go sit on the sofa with some of my dad's homemade gløgg. It's pretty lethal."

❋

Oskar tries to smile again, but his teeth are stuck to his tongue. His mouth is dry, and his hands are clenching into fists.

Erik wraps his arms around him. Rubs his hands over his back, steady, hard strokes through his thick jacket.

"I've got you, Oskar. I've got your back. Always."

ELEVEN

To be honest, Oskar doesn't know what he's worried about. Not with the smells from the kitchen and the noise and the warmth that is overwhelming every sense in him. His whole body is screaming for him to run away, anywhere. Get out of this place so he can breathe. Hide. Just disappear. But he's going nowhere.

Erik's mum has talked at him nonstop for the last ten minutes while stirring meatballs in the pan in front of her with one arm, the other holding Oskar tightly in a never-ending hug. Every so often, she pauses her monologue to shout instructions at the many random people who have kissed his cheek and shaken his hand and hugged him until he was starting to panic, at which point Erik's mum pushed him into her chest and told him she would protect him from all these lunatics. And, by the way, isn't he the most handsome boy she has ever met? Then she laughs and tells Erik he has finally done good.

Oskar doesn't remember half of what she's said, just standing there being squeezed awkwardly to death by this tall woman with her hair in a messy bun on her head, who smells of baking and meatballs and a little bit of perfume and something that reminds him of home. Like one of the scented candles his mum buys online from America with weird names like Marshmallow Mistletoe and Mahogany Teakwood.

"Mum, for heaven's sake, let go of Erik's boyfriend! He's not yours to keep, however much you try to hog him."

The woman talking looks a little frightening but in a good way. She's a female version of Erik, with the same soft sheen to her hair and those stunning blue eyes.

"Hi, handsome," she purrs and gives Oskar a double-cheek kiss that completely stuns him, and he ends up with a mouthful of hair and her hands around his face. "You weren't wrong, Erik. He does look like Prince Charming."

She throws her head back with laughter and Erik...well, Erik has gone bright red, looking like he wants to die when all Oskar can do is smile. This Erik is so far removed from The King of the Plastics in 212:B that Oskar can't quite get a grasp of it all. There's nothing of that Erik here, just a tall boy with a red face and his floppy fringe covering his eyes as he nervously chews on his thumb nail and won't look in Oskar's direction. If he did, he'd find that Oskar is feeling pretty good. How can he not with all this love around him?

"I'm Elise, Erik's sister. Well, one of them. Emmy is upstairs changing the baby—you'll meet her soon. And that tall handsome thing peeling potatoes in the corner there is my hubby Geir. This one here—" She grabs one of the whirlwinds flying past by the neck of his bright Christmas jumper. "—is Ludwig. He's mine." She plants a loud kiss on his head and lets go in time for the kid to do a full-on jump into Erik's arms, screaming, "UNCLE ERII-IKKK!" at the top of his voice. Then there is another boy—"Lukas," Elise tells him—and then everyone is talking about Lukas's front tooth having fallen out,. All the while, Oskar stands in the middle of the kitchen, feeling like he's in some kind of surreal sitcom.

"Are you any good at building Lego?" a little voice asks from behind him. It's a girl, he assumes, from her long hair. She's wearing a Batman costume and holding a box of some kind of purply Lego construction with sparkly glitter things and what Oskar thinks might be fairies. Or elves.

"Yeah?" he says uncertainly.

"Good. Then you can help me," she says and drags him off into the hallway.

Oskar hasn't seen the rest of the house, but the living room is a large open-plan with a Christmas tree and more candles and random decorations. Knitted Santas share the sofa with an elderly man, who is snoring loudly, a surly teenager in a black hoodie, who is on his phone under a blanket, and a man who rises and shakes

Oskar's hand with a cheerful, "Holger, Emmy's hubby," as the girl tugs at him to sit on the floor.

"I'm only six, so I can't read the instructions," she says, and holds the box up to Oskar to open. "You have to help me."

"You don't need to read Lego instructions, idiot," the teenager grunts, and Oskar twists the box around nervously. He can't even figure out how to open it.

"There." The girl points.

Ah. Open here.

"Are you Erik's boyfriend?" the teenager asks. He doesn't even look up from his phone, just keeps tapping away with his thumb.

"We live next door to each other. Or at least, his dorm is upstairs from mine. Kind of," Oskar says, then goes quiet.

"Cool!" The kid sighs. "Are you gay? I suppose you must be if you're his boyfriend."

"Linus!!" the man—Holger?—shouts. "That's an intrusive question to ask. Love is love, whatever we call it. Granny will be so cross if she hears you speaking to Oskar like that."

"Granny is pansexual, she told me. And she says we should ask questions if we have them. It's bad for the soul to keep secrets, she says." Linus doesn't once look up from his phone, and Oskar doesn't know what to say.

"Sorry about Linus." Holger looks genuinely mortified. "He's very direct. It's a Hansen trait. Just like his mother. Have you met Emmy yet?"

Oskar shakes his head knowing full well that his cheeks are burning.

"My wife is a police investigator. No stone left unturned. I hope Erik warned you about her. She'll probably drag you off to a corner at some point and hook you up to a lie detector, then ask you about your intentions with her brother. It's just who she is." Holger shrugs and turns back to the TV, where a ski-jumper spectacularly barrels into a pile of snow in a festive Eurosport medley of 'Best Ski-jump Crashes of the Year', accompanied by some festive one-hit wonder.

"Oskar! Concentrate! I found the head! This is the chief elf. She's called Star, I decided. I want to be called Star. Or Sparkle.

Which do you prefer? Star or Sparkle?" The little girl tugs at his arm and holds up a deranged-looking Lego elf, complete with pointy ears and pink hair.

"What's your name? Your real name?" Oskar tries to sound calm and cheerful when in truth he's scrambling to gather his thoughts. His brain's all over the place, and his hands are shaking again.

"Emilia! We all have names starting with E or L. It's soooo boooring."

"E names are awesome," Erik says and throws himself on the sofa next to the elderly man, who wakes up with a cough.

"Hey Uncle A! Whassup?" Erik fist-bumps the man, who could actually be Santa, with his deep belly laugh, warm smile and twinkly eyes under thick-rimmed glasses perched on his nose.

"Oh, same, same, my boy. How is university treating you?"

"All good. All good." Erik smiles at Oskar. Nods. Does that little look—the one where he checks if Oskar is okay.

"And the young man on the floor here…" Uncle Asbjørn chuckles. "Is this your Disney Prince? The golden-haired boy you have your heart set on?"

And suddenly, Erik looks like he wants to die. His face crunches up in embarrassment and fear, as if his clothes have disappeared and he's stark naked on the sofa for the world to see.

"You're right, he's a handsome boy." Uncle Asbjørn chuckles again. "Now, Erik, be a good lad and go get me a cup of your dad's gløgg. I could do with one before dinner. Is that ham cooked yet?" Then he points at the TV, where another skier has just crashed and burned. "Hooo, that one will have hurt!"

❄

I lasted an hour, Erik thinks. Not even that long. He didn't even get one hour of pretending everything was fine in the world before he was outed, his feelings laid bare. Before things went to shit, and Oskar stared at him as if to say, "What the fuck is wrong with you, man? What the hell is going on?"

In this Bed of Snowflakes We Lie

❄

Somehow, as if by magic, they all fit around the table in the kitchen. Oskar gets squeezed in between Emilia and Lukas or Ludwig or whatever the kid's name is. Frankly, he's struggling with all the names, but everyone is talking nonstop, so he feels okay. He's not expected to talk, he doesn't think. It's acceptable to just sit here and follow the conversation that criss-crosses the table like a ping-pong match. The topics change with each bowl of food that is passed around, and there are candles in every window. Christmas music plays softly in the background, and across the table, Erik…looks like someone has died.

Oskar tries. He tries to catch his eye, but he keeps chickening out and looking away when Erik occasionally glances his way. He doesn't know fuck right now. Doesn't understand anything.

He doesn't get why Erik's family seem to know all these things that Oskar doesn't know. Are they boyfriends? Is that even a thing? And when the hell did that happen? Because, as far as Oskar knows, Erik's into girls. Isn't he?

He shakes his head in frustration and fields the occasional questions thrown at him. Second year medical. Not sure what direction he'll take. Is thinking about dermatology. No, he hasn't done an autopsy or seen any dead people. Not yet. No. Awkwardly discusses alternative therapies with who he thinks is Emmy's husband and laughs with everyone else at Elise's stories. She's a high school counsellor, and her job consists mostly of dealing with misguided teenagers trying to be gangland heroes and ending up in her office crying in shame.

She's funny, loud and theatrical, whereas Emmy is quieter with a firm stare. Like she undresses you with her eyes and makes you spill every secret in your head. Oskar nods, hoping he is polite as plates get cleared and the discussion moves on to the royal family and the outrageous price of petrol, all in the same sentence.

The kids have disappeared from the table, and Oskar shuffles over when Erik moves to the chair next to him to make space for his mum's 'epic gingerbread loaf cake', which, apparently, has a coin hidden inside it. Whoever receives the slice with the coin gets the first Christmas present of the year. "And it's usually epic too," Linus declares, still nose-deep in his phone.

Erik doesn't speak. He sits there, breathing quietly and chewing on that damn fingernail. Erik, who has spent the whole afternoon making Oskar calm, hugging him and talking to him and making everything seem so easy, looks broken.

Oskar reaches out. He doesn't know what he means to do, but he reaches under the table, finds the hand resting on Erik's leg and awkwardly places his hand on top, feeling the soft skin underneath his palm.

He hasn't really thought this through. It's not like he can ask. It's not like he and Erik speak about things like this. They barely know each other. *Fuck*, he barely knows this guy at all. Yet here he is, sitting in the warmth of a family kitchen, laughing along with this woman who is literally howling over an American tourist coming into her shop, wanting to buy a moose. Not one of the many souvenir moose made by local craftsmen that Erik's mum speaks of so highly. No, this woman wanted to buy an actual, live moose. Thought it would make an excellent exotic pet for her ranch in Texas.

From a *gift* shop.

Erik's mum even does the American accent, apologising for her poor theatrical skills and reassuring everyone that she adores the American tourists, but this one had clearly lost the plot.

Oskar tangles his fingers in Erik's grip, stroking the outside of Erik's hand with his thumb.

And finally, Erik exhales, a long, drawn-out breath, and the tension in his shoulders seems to sink into the chair beneath him.

"Thank God for that, baby boy." Erik's mum reaches over and caresses his cheek. "Whatever was worrying you was turning your aura all fuzzy. It's better now. Much better, darling. Oskar, he needs you. I can tell. You are *so* good for him. I've just met you, but I see it. You are exactly like Erik described you."

She smiles at him—a smile that makes Oskar's stomach all warm.

"How did he describe me?" he asks quietly. He doesn't dare look at Erik. He can barely look up from the plateful of crumbs in front of him, his whole body tense.

"He said you were perfect, and I agree. You are pretty perfect, darling boy."

TWELVE

Erik wonders if this was a big mistake. It's not the first time he's taken a situation, turned it into something completely different in his head and then run headfirst into a mess of a shitstorm that will end in an epic crash and burn. There is no doubt about it.

He sees Oskar. He does. He knows Oskar gets anxious in social situations, and Erik's family is a lot to deal with, however lovely and funny and wonderful they all are.

Oskar has done well. Erik sees how Oskar keeps watching him, then averting his gaze when he looks back. How the frown lines on his forehead are deep cuts in his skin. How his thoughts are churning in his head like rollercoasters, up and down, one minute normal, the next panic-stricken.

At least he's holding his hand, grounding Erik into the soil of the earth like a stake until every single worry in his mind disappears. When Oskar strokes his skin, Erik has to really control himself so he doesn't purr like a cat or burst into tears. All he wants to do is throw his arms around Oskar and bury his face in his neck.

It's so bloody confusing.

Love is supposed to be easy. You're supposed to find that one person and fall in love, and then you hold each other and kiss and live happily ever after.

Well, Erik has ended up in the wrong bloody love story. He's stuck in the one full of angst and worries and confusion and pain. Lots of pain.

He has asked the universe for this. Begged for it—prayed that whoever was in charge up there would find him someone who would make him feel like this.

Desperate.

He can't even think straight as he helps his dad clear the table, loading things randomly in the dishwasher while his dad chuckles softly and removes the packet of butter Erik mindlessly places in the basket next to the dirty dishes.

"Erik, go up to bed. You're shattered. Enough." His dad strokes his cheek. Ruffles his hair.

"Yeah. Maybe." Erik hasn't thought that far ahead. He was so excited about bringing Oskar home and doing something nice for him. This Christmas was going to be epic. After all, it's perfectly normal to bring a friend home and hang out and do lots of silly things at Christmas. It's cool. It's normal.

What is not so normal is what Erik has totally brought on himself. He's aware that all he's talked about for the last six months is…well…Oskar. He's told his family everything about Oskar. Constantly. Everyone knows.

Except Oskar.

Erik is an idiot. Fact. What the hell is he thinking?

All that remains now is for Oskar to tap Erik on the arm. Three times. *Tap, tap, tap*, and it will all be over. He promised, and Erik is good at keeping promises. If Oskar's freaking out, Erik will take him home. Tuck him up in his own bed and make everything go away. He promised. He has no choice.

Hunching over the kitchen sink, he breathes slowly, hoping he can get a few more minutes. Just a little while longer, maybe time enough to get Oskar alone and try to explain the mess he has created.

But what is there to explain? *"I have the biggest crush on you. I've practically stalked you for the last six months. Hell, I've pretty much kept tabs on you since the first day I saw you because you did something to my stomach and made me realise that, yup. I wasn't straight at all. Not that this was news to me, really, but hey, do you want to be my first? Because there's nobody I would rather get naked with and try out all those things with than you. The most beautiful boy in the world. And, by the way, I really want to suck your dick. Like, yesterday."*

No. Erik needs to shut the fuck up and try to behave like a normal human being. He hasn't even mentioned the kissing yet. Yeah, because Erik wants to kiss Oskar. So, so much.

His body shudders as he takes another deep breath.

He can hear Oskar in the background and his mum's voice, as Oskar is once again bundled into one of his mum's hugs.

"Go take Erik to bed, Oskar. He's exhausted. And feel at home. Help yourself to anything you need."

Erik glances behind him, to where his mum is squashing Oskar, pressing him into her chest.

"I'll do some love therapy with you over Christmas." She says, squeezing Oskar's cheeks between her hands. "Because I think you might be one of those people who need a little extra love. Just to top up your reserves." His mum almost beams with love as Oskar squirms awkwardly under her assault. "You're very much loved, darling boy. There's a lot of love for you. We all love you. Any thoughts in your head right now are valid, but they are not for now. Now, you don't have to worry about a thing. Let it go. Just feel loved. That's all you need to do."

"Leila, let the poor boy go." Erik's dad laughs. "Oskar, I'm going skiing at seven. If you're up, you're welcome to come with me. I promise there'll be no awkward dad talk. I like to zone out when I ski, and Erik says you run every day, so just tag along if you want to. The weather should be good."

Oskar shrugs and nods. Attempts a smile as Erik's dad drags him into a hug.

"Go to bed, boys. See you in the morning."

It's Erik's turn, and it should be a relief sinking into his mum's hug, listening to the whispers in his ear. He is loved. He is cherished. He is important. He is so much loved. Instead, he almost pushes her away. Everything is a little too much right now.

He follows Oskar out into the hallway, grabbing his bag off the floor where he left it when they came in. His legs feel like lead, the exhaustion draining him by the second. He had this all wrong. This is all about to go to shit.

The first tap on his arm slices like a razorblade, and Oskar finally meets his eye.

THIRTEEN

"This is my room. It's not big, and the décor is still very much *Erik, aged twelve.*" He lets slip another nervous laugh. His heart is beating out of his chest. His hands, wet with perspiration.

It was just one tap. A small tap and a plea. *Let's go somewhere quiet, so I can breathe. So, I can get myself together.* It's becoming a little too much, a little bit out of control, and now Erik's breathing so fast he thinks he'll faint.

He hasn't yet, though. He managed to lead Oskar up the stairs to this corner back bedroom with the sloping roof and the Velux window and his single childhood bed with the Star Wars bedding and stupid posters on his walls. Drawings are still stuck to the wooden slats in the ceiling, and his desk still hosts his action figures. He grew up here. This was always safe. Home. Where he could be a child.

He doesn't feel like a child anymore, stuck in this state of half panic, half arousal, half just normal Nøst Hansen family life. And yeah, he knows that doesn't add up.

"You can have the bed. It's pretty comfy—sorry about the Star Wars covers. I do have some plain bedding, but Mum likes to tease me and make it up with the ones from when I was little." Erik rambles on as he places his bag on the desk and digs out his toothbrush. "At least we didn't get the Bamse Bear sheets. I'm sure she will dig them out for next time."

"Where are you going to sleep?" Oskar asks, removing and casting aside his jumper.

"Oh, I'll just kip on the floor."

"No," Oskar says. "No."

Erik looks at him, takes in his stubborn pose—the hands defiantly gripping the edge of his T-shirt as he pulls it over his head, and...

The swallow that comes from Erik's throat is loud. Embarrassingly loud. There is too much skin. Too much pale, perfect, soft skin.

Oskar sits on the edge of the bed and extracts a clean T-shirt from his bag, and Erik swallows again as the cotton fabric slides down Oskar's chest.

"Sleep with me," he says, tugging his sleeves straight. "We should both fit."

"Are you sure?" Erik isn't. He doesn't think he'll be sure of anything ever again.

Oskar nods and stands, unfastening and kicking off his jeans. He leaves them in a pile on the floor and digs in his bag again, pulling out a pair of raggedy, threadbare pyjama pants. They look lovely, soft, the kind of thing Erik would wear.

He has to look away, because Oskar, his Oskar, is changing into his pyjamas like it's nothing, while Erik's head is all over the place. He's feeling a little bit faint again—no wonder, since all the blood in his body is rushing to his groin like there are free prizes down there or something. Trying to push out the dirty thoughts, he turns away and quickly changes out of his clothes, which is stupid because how is he going to hide his arousal in Captain America pyjamas? He looks to his plastic mates on the desk for help.

He needs to fix this shit. Turn his room into something half adult. Not that he is an adult. *Breathe...* He takes a moment to steady himself, then turns back, keeping his eyes on the floor as he prepares to face Oskar again, calmly, sensibly, and it might even have worked, except Oskar's taken off his socks.

Fuck. His feet are beautiful. Erik shudders. *Snap out of it. Quick.*

"I should probably apologise to you for my family." He still doesn't know where to start, how to even *try* to explain, because his family isn't the problem. "None of them have any filter. They all just speak without thinking first. But—actually, no. I'm not going to apologise for them. My family is awesome. They always support me in whatever I want to do, and they've never made me feel bad about who I am. I'm a total mess, Oskar, but…I am me."

❋

"You? A mess?" Oskar has no idea where his bravery is coming from. He's never like this, but Erik feels safe. Erik, who has his heart set on him. Erik, who is apparently his boyfriend. Erik, who by all accounts has some kind of thing for him. And weirdly, that is fine. More than fine. Oskar is warm and happy and a tiny bit…embarrassed is not the word. It's more like he doesn't know what to do about it.

He sighs, takes a deep breath and continues. "Erik, you're the cool, perfect, popular dude every girl wants to score with and every bloke wants as his best mate. Everyone wants you at their party and looks at you like you're some kind of…I don't know. But you're one of the lucky ones. How on earth can you think you're a mess?" Oskar stops to breathe. *In. Out. In Out.*

He can feel the panic coming back, slowly brewing in his chest. *In. Out. IN. OUT.* If he could just grab his trainers and run for a while, he could probably make sense of the world. Or maybe lie down in a dark room on his own and watch Netflix for five hours straight, so he could get his brain to take a rest.

"I put you in an awkward situation with my family. I didn't mean for that to happen. I didn't think they would…out me like that. I thought we'd have a bit of time to hang out, so I could tell you. Or actually…I don't know what I was thinking. I just wanted to get to know you. I really wanted to spend Christmas with you. That's all I wanted." Erik sits on the bed next to Oskar, fiddling with the toothbrush in his hand.

"That's okay," Oskar says softly, surprised to find he's already calming down. It's like Erik has some kind of magic powers. He sits next to Oskar and everything is right in the world. It's a little bit strange. In a good way.

He reaches down and fishes his toothbrush from the bag and says, "Shall we go and brush our teeth?" like it's the most natural thing in the world. Like this is his life now. Like he has someone to brush his teeth with.

"Let's," Erik replies with a grin.

They stand there next to each other in the harsh light above the bathroom mirror, Erik brushing vigorously, Oskar leaning back against the sink. It's fine. It's absolutely fine.

Oskar doesn't know who giggles first, but it starts with a small burst of laughter, venting some of the tension that has built up during the day. It's freeing.

Further bursts of giggles and toothpaste bubbles spill out of Erik's mouth before he spits into the sink and says to Oskar's reflection, "Bear with my mum and the love-therapy thing. It's one of her quirks. She's really into it at the moment. Says it can cure anything. She means well, I promise."

Another explosion of laughter is brewing in Oskar's chest because this entire situation is absurd. Amazing, but absurd, and he really can't look at Erik right now. If he does, he'll go red and rip into another fit of giggles, so he bends to rinse his mouth in the sink and blurts out, "Your mum is cool," with his face in the towel. He chances a peek at Erik and adds, "The love-therapy thing is…interesting?"

"Yeah." Erik snorts at Oskar's description and leaves his toothbrush on the side. "I bet your parents are nice and normal compared to mine."

"Nah. They're just as deranged as yours," Oskar says, sending them both into reels of giggles again.

It feels good to laugh. Everything is quite good right now.

FOURTEEN

It's funny how crawling under the thin, old duvet of his childhood bed makes Erik feel small, like he is once again a little kid waiting for his parents to come in and read him his bedtime story. He shuffles over until he is right against the wall, holding up the duvet as Oskar sits and quietly swings his legs up on the bed.

"It's nothing like yours," Erik moans. It's not. Not even remotely like it.

"You and your thing for my bed," Oskar starts, then stops as if he's had second thoughts about saying what he was going to. Erik wants to ask, but he isn't brave enough to go there yet. To talk about the real things. Like feelings. So he stays quiet while Oskar stretches out beside him, shoulder to shoulder, and pulls the duvet up to his chin.

They're both far too tall for this bed, and another round of giggles ensues when their bare toes poke out at the edge of the duvet, both of them wriggling in an effort to fully cover up in a bed that is clearly too small.

It gets easier when Erik turns off the light. The darkness adds another layer of safety. Nobody can see his face or watch the way his eyes flicker, see the uncertainty in his gaze. No, darkness is good. Safe.

"I love this roof window." Briefly, he frees his arm to point up at it. "I used to lie here for hours watching the raindrops trickle down the glass, and when it snows, it takes ages for the snow to settle. Sometimes it covers the whole pane, and then suddenly it slides off and starts again. It's mesmerising."

There is only snow on the roof window now. Thick and white against the glass. Even in the dark.

They lie there in silence. Just quiet breaths and unspoken words. So many questions in Erik's head he's convinced it'll explode if he doesn't say something. But what can he say? How does he tell someone that he not only has the biggest crush on them, but that his whole world has been revolving around them since the first time he saw them? He's never done this before—spoken the truth. He always has the little lines ready…

You're really hot. Fit. Gorgeous.
You're beautiful, but you're just not for me.
It's me, not you.

He's used every single cliché, every line in the book of crap excuses, but he's never had to say what he really feels.

Until now.

And now he doesn't have the words. He doesn't know how to do this right, do it gently and safely so he doesn't scare Oskar away, but he needs to tell him. He wants Oskar to know how he feels.

Well, Oskar kind of knows already, doesn't he? His family made sure of that, but Erik wants to say it himself.

"I keep getting all their names mixed up," Oskar says into the darkness as if he's picked up on Erik's train of thought. "There are so many of them, and all the Ls and Es are confusing."

It's a safer topic, and Erik grasps it gladly.

"Mum is Leila, Dad is Einar. That's where the thing with the Ls and Es came from. They met at a party in their twenties. Mum was there with her girlfriend at the time, and Dad had this great epiphany that she was the love of his life. Probably fuelled by copious amounts of chemicals and alcohol, but hey, they married a year later. Mum is still best friends with Auntie Soraya. She's really funny—into all the same things as Mum. She walks through the door and starts reading your palm and aligning your chakra before she even has her boots off. Anyway, Mum named us all E names, after Dad, and then Emmy met Holger at uni, and they went with the Ls for their kids in homage to Mum. Linus was born when they were still living in a uni dorm in Trondheim, and Lukas came along a few years later. Then the baby is Lottie. She's bloody gorgeous. You'll meet her tomorrow."

"So Ludwig and Emilia are Elise's? And who is she married to?"

"Geir. Elise and Geir went to school together. They've known each other since they were five or something. When they were teenagers, Elise had all these boyfriends, and every weekend, Geir would come and sit on our sofa and sulk while Elise was out at parties and things. Knowing what I know now, I think he was really down most of the time, because he was in love with Elise and she couldn't stand the sight of him. She'd come home and roll her eyes at him, and he'd cross his arms and stare at her and get his shoes and slam the door as he left." He has to stop and breathe, but talking feels good so he just rambles on.

"I never really understood it back then, but I grew up with Geir, pretty much spending every weekend here, and I liked the company. Elise called him her stalker. She teased him mercilessly—she was honestly quite evil to him, and Mum would get so cross at her. Anyway. One night, Elise came home heartbroken because some shithead had dumped her, and Geir was here, and she apparently took pity on him and dragged him up to her room, and the rest is history."

"One night? That's all it took?" Oskar laughs, his body jerking softly against Erik's shoulder.

"Yup. He must have really impressed her that night. Gone all out and such."

"And Uncle Asbjørn?"

"Mum's brother. Awesome dude. He's worked all over the world as a stylist. He's worked with some seriously cool and famous people too. Ask and he'll tell you loads of amazing stories of places he's been and people he's met and things he used to get up to. You'll like him. We lost Auntie Unni a few years ago. She was really funny. Loved us all to bits."

They grow quiet again. Just lying there listening to each other breathing, shuffling awkwardly every so often.

Erik hopes Oskar will ask something else and tries to think of something safe to ask himself—something they can laugh about. Something easy.

Oskar gasps, like he is about to speak, but he swallows whatever he was going to say and the silence resumes. The only sounds lingering being soft breaths and the rumble of people left milling around downstairs.

"This isn't going to work," Oskar says eventually and shuffles his hips. "We're never going to get to sleep like this."

Erik agrees. The pillows are too thin, the duvet too short, the bed too narrow, his head too full of thoughts.

"Roll over on your side," Oskar demands, half sitting up leaning on his elbow. Erik rolls. It's not like he has a choice, although his brain is repeating *please stay, please let me stay*, over and over again, like a mantra.

He folds his pillow in half and stuffs it under his head, then folds his arms across his chest and leans his forehead against the wall. The edges of the wallpaper are still rugged from where he picked at it when he was little and sad and couldn't sleep.

Oskar shuffles closer, positioning the duvet over them both. His legs curl up behind Erik's, and he pushes his pillow against the headboard. His breathing is a little fast, his arm a little shaky as it settles around Erik's waist.

Erik can't stop smiling. He is smiling so hard his cheeks ache. If he didn't know better, he'd think the wetness at the corners of his eyes was tears. Little pools of relief and happiness and amazement that freefall down his cheeks when he blinks.

He catches Oskar's fingers with his own as Oskar's head comes to rest against his neck. Erik can feel Oskar's nose at the top of his spine, the warmth of Oskar's breath spreading across his shoulders, then the final shuffle as their chests line up and Oskar curls in around him. Spoons him, as his fingers grip Erik's hand and cold toes encounter the backs of Erik's ankles.

It's dizzying. Amazing. All consuming.

❉

Oskar is still holding his breath, hoping this is okay. Hoping that Erik will let him. Because he wants to. Goddamn, he wants to. He doesn't understand where all this need to touch has come from, the desperate urge for contact. It's almost like Erik's mum's love therapy is already rubbing off on him, and his brain has gone to mush. Well, he needs his head examined or for someone to give him a good slap so he can snap out of whatever this is…this thing has got himself into.

All this love has made him a little reckless, he thinks, and he'll probably regret it in the morning. Wake up and be all awkward, and things will be weird. But for now, it's pretty much perfect.

He squeezes Erik's hand a final time. "Night, night, Erik from Upstairs."

Erik tugs at his hand, moves it up slightly so it is right over his heart, *thump, thump, thump* under Oskar's wrist.

In for a penny and all that, Oskar snuggles closer. He might as well. Because this. This here—

"Night, night, my Disney Prince," Erik whispers.

This is what dreams are made of.

FIFTEEN

There is a soft tap on the sole of his foot. And another.

"Oskar!"

Tap. Tap. Tap. Tap.

Oskar jerks out of sleep and stares awkwardly at Erik's dad, who is standing next to the bed, placing a cup of something steaming hot on the desk.

"I'm just getting dressed now. Get yourself ready to leave in about fifteen minutes. The weather is perfect. It's snowing again, and it's great conditions out there."

Oskar means to counter that with a complaint that it's the middle of the night and it's Christmas and he's quite warm and comfortable, thank you very much, although his T-shirt is soaked with sweat from being plastered to Erik's back for most of the night, so he smiles and nods and hopes Erik's dad will get the message and leave.

"Hot lemon and ginger. It'll get your blood flowing and wake you up a bit. I'll see you outside."

Another nod. Erik snuffles in his sleep and tugs at the duvet.

It's tempting. Really tempting to curl back around Erik and revel in having someone in his arms. Addictive is probably the right word. He never wants to sleep alone, ever again. Erik is warm and soft and smells like toffee and hugs and Christmas and toothpaste and some shampoo that Oskar needs to buy so he can just sit and sniff it all day long like the junkie he is.

Because Erik is kind of addictive. There's no question about that.

But he needs to run. He'll feel much better if he can get an hour. Even half an hour would clear the murky mess of thoughts clouding his brain right now. Well, half of it is a murky mess; the rest is, quite frankly, a little bit terrifying. Oskar doesn't even want to acknowledge that he's actually thinking about it. That he's admitting to himself this is something he feels. And that he is okay with it. He is strangely fine with it all. He thinks.

Well, everything is fine while they're here in this strange house of hugs and smells and people and children and noises. *And bloody Star Wars*, he thinks as he knocks over a Darth Vader figurine that was precariously leaning against the desk lamp. He almost swears out loud as he scalds his lips on the rim of the mug of boiling liquid. It's probably some magic potion. Some Nøst Hansen secret weapon to make everyone fall in love with them before they take them out onto the forest trail behind the house and murder them with an axe.

He still gets dressed, feeling the calmness descend on him as he pulls the tight spandex over his legs, zips up his windproof, lightweight running jacket and pulls a hat over his head. His headphones are around his neck, his thick socks straining over his toes.

Yup, he is definitely the idiot in the horror movie who walks straight into the trap and meets his sticky end. He laughs to himself as he steps outside into the frosty morning. It's still pitch-dark, and Erik's dad is stepping into his skis, shaking the snow off the poles. He's right, though. It's pretty perfect, eerily quiet, the soft fall of flakes from the sky flanked by the streetlights.

"There is a head torch on the side there if you want it, but the trail is floodlit all the way around, so I usually go without." Erik's dad is stretching his legs, bouncing on his heels as he speaks.

Oskar flexes his feet, gently bending his knees as he fastens his gloves around his wrists.

"Shall we?" Erik's dad asks.

"Let's go," Oskar replies.

Thirty minutes later, they're back on the steps, Oskar panting like he has run a bloody marathon and Erik's dad laughing softly as he taps his skis off.

"You're a good runner, kiddo. Fast," he says, giving Oskar an appreciative smile.

"You're a fast skier," Oskar admits. "I struggled to keep up."

Honestly, his knees are singing, and his lungs are still pushing his breaths out a little too fast under his jacket, which is suddenly restrictive and hot, and there are all these things in his head fighting to get out. It's a little dizzying, the things he wants to do. Right now, all he can think of is running upstairs and lying down next to Erik, telling him about the graceful hares that crossed the tracks in front of them, the flurries of snow drifting across the fields like fairy dust, the majestic moose that stood in the clearing as they descended the last hill, the sound of the water trickling down through the lumps of ice under the bridge.

He wants to tell Erik that he loves all this—the quietness and total peace of early mornings when you are the only one there. When you can just run and feel and see and watch the snowflakes randomly forming shapes in your line of sight as you push through the pain and breathe hard, your muscles burning as you reach the top of that hill.

Erik's dad kept his promise delivering no awkward dad talk. Just a silent wave of his ski pole to turn, an open hand to stop and an appreciative glance as Oskar finally overtook him on the last straight coming out of the clearing on the home run. It was nice to have some no-pressure company, just a companion doing this for the same reason Oskar does it. To give his brain a break. To stop the thinking. To let himself drown in the music that pounds in his ears. It's freeing. Liberating.

And it fucks with his knees, he thinks, as he stumbles to the kitchen sink and grabs a glass off the draining board, filling it repeatedly and letting the cool water slide down his throat until his body regains its composure.

"Thank God, you're up! Brilliant. Oskar. Favour. Take Lottie off me for a second."

Emmy is zipping her coat and throwing a wrap around her neck as Oskar awkwardly takes the wriggling infant from her and tries to hold her away from his soaking jacket.

"Da-da-da-dadada-daaaa." Lottie coos and seizes a handful of Oskar's hair in her grabby little hand. She tugs and giggles, and a dollop of drool escapes from her mouth and starts its slow descent down her chin. Oskar can deal with babies. Tiny versions of humans who don't talk. Perfect.

"We need to do a stealth coffee run before Mum wakes up. Do. Not. Breathe. A. Word to her if she comes down. As far as she's concerned, you know nothing. Just come down to the garage in twenty minutes, yes?" She pulls her hat over her head. "Geir and Holger are starting the car down the road. You've seen nothing. You have no idea where I am. You're just playing with Lottie. Totally normal."

She winks and sneaks out the door, closing it carefully behind her.

They are clearly all nuts, this family. Oskar has never seen anything like it.

He needs a shower. He needs…honestly, he doesn't know what the hell he needs. But that's fine. He hoists Lottie onto his hip and stands over by the living room window, watching the birds peck at the bird table. The light is slowly creeping up over the top of the trees in the distance.

"Shall we be friends?" he whispers to Lottie. This human is safe. Definitely safe. As long as he holds her and shakes her around a little bit and does the occasional appropriate coos, she seems to be happy.

"Daddadadad-daaa. Iiiikkk!" She dribbles back, blowing bubbles and spit at him. She's cute.

The house is silent around him, the odd creak of wood breaking through every so often along with his socked footfalls on the hard floors. The Santas on the sofa are watching him with their smug smiles. Half the cushions from the chairs are still on the floor from last night where the boys had been watching TV.

He wonders what his own parents would make of this if they'd come along for Christmas with the Nøst Hansens. He thinks his dad would be fine with it all. He'd probably enjoy the sport on TV, the long-winded board games and the kids roaming around.

His mum, though…Oskar smiles, thinking how much she'd love this. First, she'd take Erik's mum and her love therapy thing and over-analyse it to death. Bring her laptop to the table and pull up research papers arguing fact versus fiction and proven medicinal research and clinical trials versus alternative therapies and nontraditional cures. She lives for those kinds of things. Funnily enough, he thinks Erik's mum would hold her own and smother his mum in hugs and cuddles until she held her hands in the air announcing defeat while suggesting a year-long study to prove her point.

His mum is the most stubborn woman in the world, despite her constant fears of not being good enough, posh and polished enough and, of course, never perfect enough. His feeling is that Erik's mum is nothing like that. She just takes the world for what it is and doesn't give a crap what anyone else thinks. Two women carrying the same passionate beliefs but channelling them in wildly different ways.

There is movement from the basement, and Oskar shifts Lottie to his other hip so he can hold on to the railings as he carefully negotiates the steep stairs down. He can hear quiet voices and muffled laughter as he follows the sounds and carefully opens the door to what looks like a garage.

"Oskar! Come in," Holger whispers a little louder than he should. Emmy and Geir seem to be giddy with giggles, lining up takeaway cups from the local coffee chain on the workbench in the corner and setting up garden chairs on the concrete floor.

The door creaks behind them, and Linus pops his head around the door. "Yay! Stealth Coffee Club is ON!" He fist-pumps in the air, and Emmy hands him a cup while ruffling his hair and trying to sneak a kiss to his cheek.

"Merry Christmas, Mummy's beautiful boy," she coos as Linus blushes in embarrassment.

"Oskar, black coffee, right? I did ask Erik, so we were prepared. Welcome to the Stealth Coffee Club, the most exclusive of the Nøst Hansen secret societies." Holger laughs quietly and takes a sip from his cup, closing his eyes in delight.

"There are rules to this Stealth Coffee Club, Oskar. Listen carefully." Linus looks stern, yet his face is full of laughter. "The first rule of Stealth Coffee Club is…you do not talk about Stealth Coffee Club. Is that clear?"

"Crystal." Oskar laughs back and manages to sit in the rickety garden chair behind him, balancing Lottie on his lap and the coffee in his hand.

"Second rule of Stealth Coffee Club." Geir also tries to look serious but fails on account of the foam moustache on his top lip. "Stealth Coffee Club does not exist. No caffeine ever crosses the threshold into this house. Seriously. It is evil and will make you a bad human being. But nobody ever said we can't drink coffee in the garage. So this is where we get our fix. In secret. Do *not* tell Leila. If you even mention the word coffee upstairs, you will be shot at dawn. With Lukas's Nerf gun. Seriously, Oskar, your place in this family depends on your discretion."

"And we will not let you play 'Settlers' later." Linus pretends to shoot him with his finger gun. Oskar would shoot back, but he has his hands full. He nods instead.

The door behind them creeps open, and Uncle Asbjørn hobbles in, shuffling in his slippers with a blanket over his shoulders.

"Desperate times, desperate measures," he pants as Emmy grabs his arm and helps him sit down.

"Merry Christmas, Uncle A." Geir laughs and hands him a cup. "Double espresso, two sweeteners."

"Thank God, darling boy, I was getting the shakes up there! Oskar! Welcome to the bad coffee club. Or…what is it we call this?"

"Stealth Coffee Club," Holger says.

"Third rule of Stealth Coffee Club," Linus adds, looking very pleased with himself, "is for God's sake, do not tell Granny that there is caffeine in chocolate. Because if she finds out we will all be fucked forever and ever, Amen." Erik sneaks in behind them, closing the door with a quiet click.

"AMEN!" they all shout in unison.

"It's like church." Uncle Asbjørn chuckles. "But with much better coffee, comfier chairs and the best company in the world. Thank God I have you lot. I would have a caffeine-withdrawal-induced heart attack if you didn't rescue me in the mornings."

"Best part of Christmas, this," Holger declares, clasping his cup like it's precious, the steam clouding the glasses on his nose.

Erik is hobbling around in his socks, lifting the lids on the remaining cups. "Which one's mine, Em?"

"Left." Emmy gives Erik a hug. "Gingerbread caramel latte with cream and sprinkles."

"Epic." Erik leans against the workbench, taking a satisfying sip of his coffee, and winks at Oskar, whose stomach goes all warm.

Oskar grins like an idiot, while Lottie kicks her legs and tries to grab hold of his hair again.

"She likes you," Erik says.

"She's my new friend." Oskar laughs and drags her back up onto his lap. "She's a wriggly little thing."

"Merry Christmas." The voice behind them bellows, making everyone turn around, shushing desperately. "Don't worry. Mum's in the shower. We have at least five minutes. Which one's mine?" Erik's dad is almost shaking with anticipation as he grabs the cup from Emmy.

"Oh Dad, you poor thing."

Erik's dad shrugs cheerfully. "I get to have a coffee once a year with my family. I can live the rest of the year without it as long as it makes your mother happy. And Erik, your boy Oskar can run. You weren't wrong about that. I'll take you up the other trail tomorrow, Oskar. There are some fun, challenging hills that way, and if we're lucky, we'll see more moose." He nods to Oskar, who is still grinning.

He can't help it. This is nothing like he imagined. Nothing like the Christmases he grew up with. All these people hiding in the cold garage with their coffees, Uncle A and his deep belly laugh teasing Holger for something. Emmy not even attempting to remove the baby from his lap, and Erik, who just stands there, leaning against some rickety workbench looking totally relaxed and watching him with a tiny smile on his face. His eyes, well, there is something about the way they watch him that Oskar can't quite get his head around. He likes it. He likes having Erik look at him like this—like he is special. Like he belongs. Like there is nowhere else Erik would rather be than in this concrete room, full of rubbish and tools and crap and people laughing over shared secrets.

"I'm so happy you're here," Erik mouths at him, and Oskar feels the blush creeping up his cheeks, the warmth in his stomach burning through his damp clothes.

"Me too," he mouths back. Right now, there is nowhere else he would rather be.

"Oi!!" Elise sticks her head around the doorframe. "Fuck, I overslept, and Mum is on her way down! Let me neck that coffee and I'll run back up and distract her!"

Oskar can't help the giggle that escapes his mouth as everyone scrambles, downing the last drops of coffee and throwing their cups into the bag Erik holds out.

"Use Mrs Amundsen's bin, she's on holiday until January. Go!" Erik's dad shakes his head and meets Oskar's eye as he pushes Erik out through the garage door. "Welcome to the family, Oskar. We're all beyond help here."

Oskar just laughs and hands Lottie back to her mum.

Somehow, he feels right at home.

Sixteen

Erik feels like he is on the top of the world one minute, his whole body buzzing with adrenaline, only for him to crash to the depths of despair the next minute over something as stupid as Oskar sitting next to Elise on the other side of the table during lunch, rather next to Erik, where he should be. Erik needs him to be there, so he can touch him, feel their thighs press close, though he does manage to reach his foot under the table and give Oskar's a gentle nudge. Oskar looks up and smiles, and wham, bam, Erik is back on cloud nine again.

It's exhausting. He is exhausted. At least Oskar escapes for a shower before they play another gruelling round of some board game, where, of course, Ludwig and Lukas win again and Erik comes last. He blames it on Oskar. Totally. Because while he should have been developing a strategy to get himself ahead in the game, he was too busy looking at Oskar's hands. Oskar has gorgeous hands, and his eyelashes flicker slightly when he's trying to concentrate, and there's a little spot on his nape where his skin dips, which Erik is now obsessed with. He wants his lips there, kissing the soft skin under the damp curls that ride the neck of Oskar's T-shirt.

This whole being in love thing is draining. Erik needs to go to bed and sleep solidly for a week. Preferably with Oskar. In Oskar's bed.

In a strange way, he wants to go and tap Oskar on the arm. Say, "Fuck this Christmas thing. I just want to lie down in a dark room with you in my arms for an hour or two until I can get myself into some sort of functioning state. Please. Just hold me and make all these doubts in my head disappear because I can't do this much longer. I can't hold it together anymore. I can't. Please."

But of course, he doesn't. He curls up on the sofa and smiles smugger than Santa on Christmas morning when Oskar joins him, tucking those long legs up under himself then leans on Erik's shoulder. Which makes Erik want to kiss him, wrap him up in an all-consuming hug and bury his face in Oskar's neck and just stay there.

It's freaking soul-destroying. Fucking hell.

✻

There has been so much food that Oskar isn't sure he'll be up for any sort of run in the morning. Breakfast was just bread and brown cheese, but Oskar has never tasted cheese like it, locally made by some farmer whose kids are in Erik's dad's class. Lunch was fantastic: the lamb sausages the best he'd ever had. Now Holger is grilling a massive slab of belly pork in the kitchen, while Geir is peeling what looks like a mountain of root vegetables, and there are Pork Patties and Christmas sausages ready in a pan, and more of that homemade bread Oskar has already had far too much of, with some amazing stinky French cheese and local butter, and it's just… *Wow.*

There is a big tray of homemade cakes on the coffee table in front of them, with gingerbread biscuits and those little fried cakes he remembers from his childhood. There are also golden crisp wafers with whipped cream, and Oskar's mouth is watering. He is not hungry, but he is definitely having one of those cream things.

Erik laughs softly in his ear. "Mum does the whole seven varieties of cakes at Christmas. There are more to come, and then she has a whole almond wreath cake for tomorrow. I'm going to feel sick later. I always do. I can't help myself."

"So, no caffeine but she kills you all off with sugar?" Oskar teases, but he knows Erik will get what he means. It's strange how comfortable he has felt all day. Accepted. Like he is one of them. When he clearly is not.

But he wants to be, and it's kind of painful to not know where he stands. Because how can he?

✻

"Yeah, funny that." Erik touches his nose to Oskar's cheek, as if he's painting a little line down through the soft stubble, and then recoils in fear. He didn't mean to do that, but it's like he can't help himself, and now Oskar is sitting there with a blush creeping over his cheeks and a cheeky smile as he licks whipped cream off his fingertip.

It's obscene. Filthy. And Erik is sporting a semi in his joggers as Oskar takes another bite of his cake leaving a tiny smidge of cream on the tip of his nose.

There are children present. His father is sitting opposite him, his cheerful laugh echoing through the room as they all watch *Donald Duck's Christmas*—a vintage collection of cartoon clips that is shown on Christmas Eve every year and is of course religiously watched by every self-respecting human who owns a TV. Uncle Asbjørn hobbles past and sits next to Oskar, the sofa creaking under his weight.

"Oh! It's Ferdinand the bull," he hums excitedly. "My favourite. Every year."

It doesn't help Erik snap out of the gruesome state he's in. If Oskar turns and looks at him right now, Erik will probably come in his pants like an out-of-control, oversexed teenager.

"Epic cakes. Best I've ever had." Oskar is still licking his fingers, then dries them on his jeans, casting a quick glance at Erik, who jerks like he's been stabbed.

"You have cream on your nose," he blurts out, trying to rescue himself and unwisely reaches out, scooping the cream off with his fingertip, imagining Oskar sucking it clean. *Fuck. This is bad.*

"PRESENTS!!!!" Ludwig shouts and does a kneeling slide across the floor, crashes into the side of the sofa and flops onto his back laughing, unwittingly rescuing Erik from his self-torture.

❄

Everyone is cheering, hastily moving up on the sofa so bums can find seats, the kids excitedly wriggling around on the floor, and baby Lottie once again gets placed on Oskar's lap. He doesn't mind, not even a little bit.

"Babies are good for the soul," Erik's mum says as she squeezes in between Oskar and Uncle Asbjørn, who is almost bouncing up and down with excitement, holding a giant black bin liner. "It is a medically proven fact that having a baby in your arms lowers your blood pressure and calms you down. However tense or anxious you may be, you will automatically direct some of your oxytocin stash towards the baby to ensure its safety. The body is quite amazing, don't you think, Oskar?"

"Really?" Oskar asks, thinking she may have a point. He pulls Lottie closer and sniffs her hair, feeling a little bit silly, but he can't help himself. He likes it almost as much as having Erik's head leaning on his shoulder, like he is now. It's comforting and does funny things to his insides, setting off the butterflies that flap around in there whenever he looks at Erik. Not that there's much fluttering room left after everything Oskar has stuffed in his mouth since breakfast.

"She likes you too, Oskar." Emmy laughs and throws herself on Holger's lap. "And honestly, it's nice to have someone to help entertain her. Gives my arms a break."

"*Silence*!!!" Uncle Asbjørn hollers, and everyone sits up straighter, giggling nervously. The children on the floor all cover their faces in anticipation.

"Thank you! Oskar, since you are the newest addition to our family, let me start by apologising. You have done nothing to deserve this." He bows his head, and everyone laughs, including Oskar, because Uncle Asbjørn looks so excited he will probably combust if he is not allowed to go on in peace.

"Oskar, I spent my entire working career dressing people, styling people for formal occasions and events. Now that I'm happily retired, I'm finally allowed to have some fun. And you lot very kindly allow me to indulge in getting back at you for all the pranks and grief you give me throughout the year. So, the yearly tradition continues as I, the great Asbjørn Hansen, stylist to the stars, get to dress you all for Christmas dinner."

He does a little bow again as the family cheer and roar.

"Last year, we all dressed as Christmas Stormtroopers," Elise explains through her laughter. "Except Mum and Dad, who were

Princess Leia and Darth Vader. It was bloody brilliant. We'll have to show you the photos.

"The year before, we were all characters from *Frozen*," Emmy continues. "I loved that. I've worn my Elsa dress to parties. It's just gorgeous." She sighs, all dreamy, while Linus actually looks up from his phone.

"My Olaf costume doesn't fit anymore. Such a shame. It was absolutely epic."

"So, what on earth have you got planned this year, Uncle A?" Erik looks a little worried, fidgeting under the cushion he has firmly wedged on his lap.

"Well, you have all been awfully brilliant this year, so I thought I'd be kind. I read somewhere about this thing called Furries."

"Fuck," Emmy blurts out. "Can I impose a total Facebook ban, please? No photos anywhere."

Elise slaps her over the head. "No swearing in front of the kids."

"It is all going on my public Insta," Uncle Asbjørn declares. "I absolutely insist! Now, back to Furries." Giggles threaten to tumble out of his mouth with every word, while Holger looks set to explode into a knitted Santa and Geir is burying his head in Elise's back.

"I've decided for this year, we should be comfortable for Christmas Dinner, so we're all going to be Furries. And before you drag me off and shout at me, we are *not* going to be the *adult* variety of Furries. There will be no X-rated action in these suits. Let me indulge you, my darlings, in the super-soft wonder that is animal onesies."

"Onesies were a thing three years ago, Uncle A," Linus says wearily.

"I know, young man, but Uncle A can do whatever he likes. So, suck it up and get dressed." He starts throwing neatly wrapped parcels around the room.

Oskar has laughed a lot in his life, but he has never laughed to the point of feeling like he's going to throw up over the baby on his lap, which is the state he's in ten minutes later. Because seriously, Erik's mum is dressed as a giant unicorn, complete with a horn on her head, and she's clearly loving it, dancing around the room with her husband, who is dressed like a giant bear. There's also a strange-looking raccoon, a giant koala, a squirrel—that's Elise—and they're all in hysterics, trying to figure out what on earth Holger is, while Geir is a spotty dog and Linus appears remarkably smug in his jet-black gorilla outfit.

Then there's Erik, so glamorous in his giraffe onesie, he should be on a catwalk in Milan. He looks pretty amazing, standing there and coolly taking in the chaos around him while everyone else is wiping their eyes and trying to gather up the masses of wrapping paper on the floor.

"So we have to wear this for dinner?" Oskar asks as he unfolds the soft, white fabric, which Lottie is trying to get her teeth into. He's quite masterfully dressed her in her ladybird onesie, and she already has one of the antennae in her mouth, the hood half covering her face as she tugs and drools and squeals.

"Nope." Linus smiles. "The rules are, you pretty much have to live in whatever Uncle A dresses you in for the rest of Christmas. Rules are rules. If you're part of this family, you must live with the fact that you can't leave the house until after New Year's because you're dressed up as something weird." He laughs evilly at Oskar. "Good luck with that, Mr Cat!"

"Remember that year when we were all dressed as cartoon superheroes? It was bloody hilarious!" Erik's dad walks over in his bear suit, like it's the most normal thing in the world, and takes Lottie from Oskar so he can put on his onesie.

Within minutes, he's transformed into giant, soft, white cat, and Emilia is jumping into his arms shouting, "We are almost twins, Oskar! I'm a tiger, and you're an arctic big cat! Like a polar cat!"

And all of a sudden, it's just a little heavy, a tiny bit too much. Overwhelmed, he hugs Uncle Asbjørn and high-fives Ludwig in his racoon onesie, all with Emilia clinging around his neck.

He needs a breather. A little space.

He looks over at Erik, who is laughing and dancing baby Lottie around the room. Erik the giraffe, who Oskar really needs to hug right now—one of his strong, all-consuming hugs where his hands never stop moving over Oskar's back and his face is buried in Oskar's neck.

Oskar's shocked when he realises that not only does he *need* one of Erik's hugs, but he also *wants* one because he likes them. He likes them so much he's shaking at the thought of stealing one—of maybe doing what Erik said and tapping him twice on the arm. Begging to be taken away from here, just for a little while, so he can calm down. Remember who he really is.

Because he has no idea who Oskar Høiland is anymore.

SEVENTEEN

In the end, Oskar doesn't have to tap Erik on the arm. He doesn't even have to ask. Erik grabs his hand, and then the two of them are running up the stairs. Erik switches on the light as they walk into his room. Oskar follows and swiftly switches it off again.

He needs the darkness to stay brave. He doesn't want to be able to see because he's about to do something reckless again. Something primal and weird and needy and desperate.

He tackles Erik against the wall, climbing into his embrace with a small growl that he couldn't hold in if he tried. He is that desperate.

He claws at Erik's back, his face somewhere in Erik's neck. He's on his tiptoes, one knee between Erik's legs, his whole body pinning Erik to the wall.

He doesn't know what's come over him or what his body's doing. He can't control shit right now. All he knows is that he needs this. He needs to be as close to Erik as physically possible, and it's frightening the strength he has in him when he really wants something.

"Shhh, baby, it's fine. I'm here," Erik whispers. He gets Oskar. He always gets Oskar. It's like he has some kind of freaky mindreading thing going on, as his hands are already on Oskar's back, delivering strong, steady strokes that make Oskar birth sounds from his throat that he can't control.

He's not crying. He's not hurt. He's just. He doesn't.

Just don't let go of me.

There's nothing graceful about how they tumble onto the bed, all legs and arms and super-soft, fleecy onesies, and Oskar can't stay still, crawling all over Erik until he's practically straddling him on the bed, and it's still not enough. It's nowhere near enough.

His brain isn't working, thank God, or he wouldn't be pulling the zip down on Erik's giraffe onesie. He wouldn't be brave enough to tug at the T-shirt he's wearing underneath. Soon, there is just skin over bones and Oskar's fingertips roam over the softness, the warmth, the slight curve where Erik's muscles attach to his ribcage.

Oskar doesn't dare to look at him. He's only half aware of his arms being freed from his cat suit, of his T-shirt being pulled over his head. He doesn't even realise his jeans are undone until warm hands softly stroke the curve of his hips and roam gently across the dip in his back.

He needs this so much.

Erik tugs at him. Strong, firm tugs until Oskar is lying flat on top of him. Chest against chest. Erik's heart pumps through them both as Oskar clings to the man underneath him and squeezes his eyes shut as his face is once again snuggly stuck in Erik's neck. Skin against skin. Warmth against warmth.

"We need to stop for a little bit," Erik whispers. "I don't want to embarrass myself, because I'm about to come in my furry suit."

Oskar doesn't know whether to laugh or cry, and he half snuffles, half giggles into Erik's neck. He holds on a little tighter, his fingers roaming Erik's hair and tickling down his shoulders. His lips touch skin, soft and dizzying under his caress. He wants to kiss, lick, taste, but he's not quite that brave yet. So he lies in a heap on top of poor Erik, who continues drawing comforting little circles over Oskar's back.

"How do you always know what I need?" Oskar whispers. "I don't even have to ask. You just take care of me when I need you."

❋

Erik wants to say, *"Because I love you."* He wants to say, *"Because you are my person. You might not know it, but you are."* These and other words are on the tip of his tongue, threatening to spill out. *"Because you make me feel like I'm okay. That it's okay to be me—as long as you're here with me, everything is fine. You make me want to be different. You make me strong. You make me feel so damn strong."*

Instead he says. "Because I do."

Having Oskar on top of him is not helping his raging boner. There is too much skin. Too much Oskar. Too much.

"Sit up, baby," he whispers and pushes up until they're both kind of half sitting, Erik all flustered and glassy eyed. Oskar is still on his lap.

❋

Oskar adds another item to the list of things he likes. He likes when Erik calls him baby. It's probably all the freaking oxytocin swirling around in his system making him soft. *Baby.* He wants to be Erik's baby. He's behaving like one, that's for sure, as he lets Erik pull the onesie back up over his shoulders. Their faces are too close. The tip of Erik's nose is millimetres from his, warm, soft breaths stroking his skin as the zip fastens underneath his chin.

"I want you so much. I want to do all these things with you, but I…" Erik looks down as his voice fades, and Oskar leans in, their foreheads resting against each other.

Oskar closes his eyes. "We don't have to do anything. Let's just sit here for a while." He wishes he had answers to all the questions that are swirling around inside his head. He wishes he knew how on earth to do this. How do you make this work? Deal with all the feelings that are paralysing his body right now? How the hell did he end up feeling all these things for a boy he hardly knows? He has more sense than this, more self-preservation than to let himself fall this carelessly into the depths of the urges that are singing in his body. Yet he wants…needs…feels…breathes.

And he knows. If he only moves a tiny little bit, just tilts his head and goes for it. It's so close. Right there in front of him. It's just skin on skin, and he's had so much of Erik's skin on his already, it shouldn't be a big deal. A mouth on a mouth. Lips on lips. Not that big of a deal, is it? Or it shouldn't be, but it feels like a mountain range building up in his mind.

He's not brave enough. Not yet. Maybe never. Just the thought of that makes his heart splinter.

❋

Erik's first kiss was the perfect first kiss. He has always thought that. He'd been sat on the beach listening to the swell as it battered the sun-kissed sand, with a girl whose name he can no longer remember, and his brain was a little fuzzy from the excitement of it all. He was fifteen, he thinks, and hadn't even questioned it. It had been sweet and innocent, soft and gorgeous, her lips softly nibbling, pressing gently against his until he was brave enough to kiss back. To taste and experiment and get it all wrong and fumble and laugh.

He walked home afterwards with his fingers tracing his lips, thinking it was a milestone, another step into adulthood, and wondering what came next. Wondering what he was missing. Wondering how to figure it all out. But he had been happy. He wouldn't change a thing.

He wants the same for Oskar—for his first kiss to be perfect too, so he can look back and think, *yes. It turned out fine. It turned out to be more than fine.*

Because Oskar confided to Erik that he's never been kissed, it's Erik's responsibility, and not his kiss to just take. Oskar has the right to make this whatever he needs it to be. It's not Erik's to steal just because he can't control himself. He needs to pace this. He needs to be patient. He...*needs.*

Fuck, he needs so much it's painful.

Instead, he wraps his arms around Oskar's shoulders and lets himself fall into the hug that Oskar so willingly gives him, melting into the comfort of having someone hold him like this. They rock together slowly, in time to some silent beat only the two of them can hear, warm breath on his neck, hands strong and firm on his back.

❋

Oskar is thinking so hard he can barely see for the flashes of emotions criss-crossing his brain.

He thinks that this might just be right. In whatever fucked-up way this has happened, this is right.

It's so right that all the doubts screaming in his head, screaming that this is fucking wrong…

Well, they can fuck right off.

EIGHTEEN

There are traditions that must be upheld. There are rules.

Not that Erik's parents have brought up him and his sisters in any kind of strict household. They were brought up to be free, to play and learn and ask questions and feel loved. Whatever happened, whatever went wrong, his parents always held him tight and stroked his hair and told him that he was loved. That sometimes life would be wonderful. Sometimes life would kick you in the balls. You just had to accept it. As long as you had your family, you were safe.

And right now, he is so incredibly grateful for his family, even if they are all squabbling playfully in the kitchen putting the final touches to dinner. His mum is kneading together another batch of gingerbread dough, since someone—she waves her ladle around the room pretending to be angry, which, while wearing a unicorn onesie, makes her look wild and unhinged—ate all the gingerbread biscuits. Well, everyone is guilty of that. Gingerbread biscuits are like crack. Once you have one, you can't stop. Like seriously, you need to eat a whole tin because anything else would just be wrong.

His dad is walking around in his bear onesie, lighting candles and humming 'Jingle Bells' under his breath. Uncle Asbjørn hobbles about, snapping photos of them all on his phone, no doubt posting them for the world to see on his Insta. And Oskar…

Oskar is alive. He's laughing and smiling and looking…Erik can't even find the words anymore.

He loves how Linus has dragged Oskar over to the kitchen table where the kids are making paper decorations for the tree. Those are the rules. Every Christmas Eve, they make a decoration each for the tree. Stupid, ugly, paper decorations that they all laugh about while drinking gløgg and talking about things they've done during the year. Then, after Christmas, his mum will take all the little crinkled decorations down and glue them into her scrapbook along with photos and mementos of the year. She likes to look back at them, stroking them with her fingers and remembering the things the children thought were important. The heroes of the moment. The little quirks.

Those are the rules. They have so many little traditions now that Christmas has almost become stressful trying to squeeze them all in. Even Holger says he wouldn't spend Christmas anywhere else, having abandoned his earlier beliefs that Swedish Christmas far outweighs Norwegian Christmas. These days, he cooks his Swedish Christmas Dinner on the 23rd, followed by Norwegian Christmas on the 24th, and then they descend into the massive mess that is commonly known as the great big leftover pile-up, which they live off until New Year's Eve, when Erik's mum declares a 'food truce' and orders them all pizza from the little restaurant down the road.

Rules are easy. This is what they do. A leads to B. B inevitably leads to C. Then C leads to the sofa, where everyone ends up in a heap full of spilled drinks and crumbs and leftover food and a midnight feast of whatever gets brought out from the kitchen. Easy. Simple.

What is not so simple is Oskar. Ever since they snuck away, arms tangled around each other, something has changed—mostly in a good way. Their fingers are still laced together, and Erik's head is still on Oskar's shoulder, his hands on Oskar's back because he doesn't dare to let go. It's like something has clicked, and if he can just keep one piece of his body latched on to Oskar's, then the world keeps spinning, slowly and steadily, and Erik can cope and breathe, and everything is chill. Easy.

Then Oskar will do something unexpected, something small, like turning to help Emilia cut something out of the paper she is holding, and Erik will lose his grip on Oskar and panic, pain shooting through his limbs until he can grapple and reach, and get his fingertips back where he needs them. When he can feel the warmth of Oskar's body through the super-soft fleece of the outlandish outfits they're wearing, he can breathe again.

For all of this, Erik still manages with shaky hands to cut out little hearts from the sparkly craft paper, criss-cross the cuts in neat rows so he can fold them together to form a little woven heart-shaped basket, like the ones they used to make at school.

It's almost symbolic this year, he thinks as he weaves the final pieces together and opens the basket, pushing gently with his fingers so it gains body in its 3D shape. Two identical flat pieces of paper, now tangled together forever in a basket full of—he has to stop and smile. He is such an emotional basket case. A romantic dork of epic proportions.

He picks up a red marker pen and writes along the bottom corner *Erik and Oskar*, with a tiny little love heart at the end. Oskar notices, of course he does, and leans in, resting his head against Erik's temple.

"Cute," he whispers.

"I know," Erik whispers back.

"I made a stick insect snow angel." Oskar giggles and holds up his attempt at an angel with its messy, thin wings and long straggly limbs made from glittery paper.

"Very you," Erik says, tracing the sharp, clean edges with his fingertip. "You're good at this."

Oskar smiles, that blush creeping up again, more noticeable than ever against his white furry hood.

"Oskar, come help me hang it on the tree." Emilia tugs at Oskar's hand as she holds up the thing she has created. Erik's not quite sure what it is, but he gets up and follows. Because not following Oskar around like a lost sheep is apparently something Erik has completely forgotten how to do. He shuffles behind him like a confused kid, hanging on to the sleeve of his onesie while Oskar lifts Emilia up to place her decoration on the tree.

"It's SpongeBob SquarePants," she declares.

"Of course it is!" Oskar says. "SpongeBob is epic. Good job, Emilia."

God, he's cute. Erik's head fills with a fresh batch of daydreams. He wants to have kids with Oskar. Little golden curls all over the place and names beginning with O, all of them, except he can't think of a single name beginning with O now, apart from Oskar.

Oh, well, they'll to be Oskar Jr. And Oskarella. Can you name a kid that?

"Your basket should go here," Oskar says, pointing at a spare branch, "next to my stick insect angel."

"Next to you," Erik slurs, still lost in his head.

"Always," Oskar says, and he sounds serious. "You and me." His face is a little red, his voice a little shaky as he meets Erik's eyes.

"Always," Erik replies. There is no doubt in his mind now. They haven't even kissed, but he can feel it, the way his heart flutters, his body filling with heat. The way his breath hitches and his fingers tingle. This. This is it. *Always*.

NINETEEN

The house is basically trashed come nine o'clock. They've had dinner and totally ruined the Christmassy set-up on the kitchen table, which is now a mess after some ill-advised food fights, and covered in dirty dishes and burned-out candles. There are white glittery-paper cut-outs all over the floor, along with masses of confetti and crumbs, and a stray wrapped toffee that Oskar quickly snaps up, unwraps and pops in Erik's mouth.

Oskar's a little bit lightheaded, a tiny bit drunk on sparkling wine and beer and schnapps and Anton Berg liqueur chocolates. That's another rule, apparently—toffees for the kids and completely inedible chocolates shaped like liqueur bottles for the adults, which Erik unwraps so they can play the game of guess the liqueur while everyone squirms in horror. Oskar gets some orange-flavoured monstrosity that he has to burn from his taste buds with a whole glass of Ludwig's pink julebrus drink. He owes Ludwig, big time. Ludwig even makes Oskar sign an IOU: *Oskar must give Ludwig a whole bottle of julebrus*, signed and sworn on a festive napkin.

Oskar's mum would have had a fit. Erik's mum just laughs and says she'll clean tomorrow—"In fact, you can all help clean tomorrow, so I can have a lie in." Everyone laughs at that.

"She's never had a lie-in in her life!" Erik tells Oskar, so that's not going to work. Holger claims he did most of the cooking and is now on a permanent 'feet up on the sofa break' until the New Year. Erik's dad says it's his house, and he'll happily pay whoever does the washing up, and Erik laughs and holds up his hands, admitting he's the baby of the family who gets away with murder. "I'll do the washing up," he says, "just not right now. I've eaten so much, I'm going to explode!"

There are more presents. Erik's mum cries a little over the heart-patterned knitted gloves that Erik and, allegedly, Oskar chose for her, and Oskar has to admit they're very suitable. Soft and gorgeous in a teal blue with bright-red hearts patterned randomly over the front. Erik's done well. But then, Erik does *everything* well. Even now when Oskar is full and dozy and tired and snuggled up on the sofa on Erik's chest with arms holding him tight and fingers roaming lazily over his back, he can't help thinking how good Erik is.

He made everything right this Christmas.

Oskar fiddles with the little gingerbread decoration in his pocket—his Christmas present from Erik. Oskar's heart sank for a second or two, until Erik had scooped his face up and sternly said, "NO! No, Oskar. You don't get to feel bad because you have nothing for me. You being here is enough, okay?"

Pulling the gift from his pocket now, he laughs at the two little gingerbread men holding hands. Some local handicraft, no doubt, but he loves it. Adores it. He will keep it forever, bring it out and let his fingers dance across the piped clay whenever he feels down or sad. No one has ever bought him a Christmas decoration before, and it's a little embarrassing how happy it makes him.

He doesn't want to think about tomorrow or of what will happen the day after that. Erik says they're going back—back to some life that seems so farfetched now, Oskar can't get his head around the idea that he could exist anywhere but here. Here is safe and warm and lovely, and he is someone's boyfriend. Here is where someone hugs him and cuddles him and looks at him like he is… Oskar giggles when it clicks. Erik looks at him like he is a prince in a fairy tale. Things like this just don't happen to people like Oskar.

Emmy and Elise round up people for another board game, and Erik drags Oskar into the kitchen and hands him a broom.

"Let's get this kitchen sorted, then we can go upstairs if you want to."

The suggestion makes Oskar blush like a child. Part of him is throbbing with excitement at the thought of going up, and, well, making out with Erik and maybe getting a little bit undressed again. The prospect is making him dizzy, like this is a thing he is into. Well, his cock is apparently *majorly* into that idea.

Oskar has a complicated relationship with his sexuality, he has always known that. He wanks over anything. Skin and thrusts and moans and looks. Sometimes it's just the way the hips are angled or the way the legs are kicking or a head thrown back in pleasure. Sometimes it can be something as unsexual as a voice in the background saying something simple—a few words of admiration, a command, a tender caress—and Oskar will shoot into his hands while groaning at his phone lying abandoned on the bed as he hobbles to the bathroom to clean himself up.

He thought if he ever got into someone sexually, it would probably be a girl because no way would any boy ever be into him. That was just so farfetched in Oskar's mind, he had pretty much suppressed the whole idea.

But he is sometimes attracted to guys. Well, he's attracted to Erik, and Erik's attracted to him, definitely. Still, Oskar can barely make sense of it. These things just doesn't happen in real life. In movies and rom coms and people's fucked-up poetry? Yes. In Oskar's pathetic excuse for a life? No. Not happening. How can it? He doesn't deserve this.

But then Oskar places a pile of dishes next to Erik, who is quietly stood at the sink, elbow-deep in soapsuds. And it's funny how Oskar just does things, almost by instinct. Because he just leans over, letting his head rest gently on Erik's shoulder, just for a second, and Erik leans back. Which makes Oskar pretty much plaster his chest across Erik's back and sink his nose into Erik's neck. He nuzzles a little. Sniffs. Smells. Brushes his top lip against the skin, the little bit that sticks up over the hood of his onesie.

"You know you said you owe me all these favours?" Oskar asks softly. He needs to continue talking before he chickens out. *Breathe, Oskar. In…Out…*

Erik sighs and leans back into him. "I owe you so many favours you need to start writing a list." He nudges Oskar's forehead with his cheek. "What do you want, baby?"

I want you to call me baby for the rest of my life. Oh God. Oskar's mind is racing again. He probably has some weird fetish where he needs Erik to wrap him up in blankets and give him a dummy and rock him to sleep or some shit to get off. *Fuck.*

"Do these favours include things like…" Oskar squirms, swallowing a bit too loudly as he wraps his arms around Erik's waist and presses his head right down inside the hood with giraffe ears. It's easier to talk when he's like this, clinging to the boy in front of him where no one can see him blushing and being pathetic.

"Anything, Oskar. Seriously. Tell me what you need, and I will give it to you, whatever it is. Promise."

"Kissing?" Oskar's mouth blurts out before he can stop it. "Can you teach me to kiss? I want to do kissing."

Fuck, he sounds like a five-year-old. This is bad. This is ridiculous. He should be swinging people over his knee and snogging like a pro, not hiding in Erik's neck and bruising him with the death grip around his hips.

"Oh God, yes please. Lots of kissing." Erik's whole body is doing that sagging-in-relief thing again, where he relaxes into Oskar, sinks into his embrace and presses against him to the point that Oskar has to let go and grab hold of the sink before they both collapse in a pile on the floor, soapsuds and all.

"Good. Kissing it is, then." Oskar laughs nervously.

"Kissing lessons." Erik giggles and rubs his cheek against Oskar's nose. "Although I've never kissed a boy before, so you'll be my first."

"I like that. We can be each other's firsts." Oskar smiles, all warm and soft and relieved and relaxed again as his arms move all over Erik's chest in strong, firm movements, just like Erik does to his back.

He's a fast learner, and he's figuring this out. He's getting good at hugs. Cuddles. He thinks he's getting good at this whole love thing too. He can definitely do this. Just a few lessons on the kissing thing, and Oskar will be off to a flying start. Because he is going to love the shit out of Erik. If this is his one chance at turning his life around and being happy, then he is fucking going all in.

"Love you," he whispers into Erik's neck before he can stop himself. Then he freezes up. He shouldn't have said that. Why the hell did he say that out loud?

❄

Erik has never spun around so fast in his life, soapsuds and a stray fork flying across the floor as he throws his arms around Oskar and squeezes him as tight as his muscles will allow.

"Fucking love you too," he almost squeals. Tears are running down his cheeks, and he can't understand why he's crying again when this is just so bloody perfect. "Love you so much," he whispers.

And Oskar holds him as the snow once again starts to fall outside the windows. Holds him close and rocks him and whispers words Erik can barely understand.

It's more than perfect. It's epic.

TWENTY

By the time the kitchen is half decent, everyone is back to raiding the fridge for leftovers and nibbles. Erik throws a pretend tantrum over the mess they're creating—*after he and Oskar have done all this cleaning up!*—and Oskar ends up in another session of love therapy before Erik rescues him from his mother's arms and pretty much drags him up the stairs.

Erik is a little bit desperate, maybe a tiny bit clingy. He wants to lie down with Oskar and kind of eat his face. Or something.

He sighs as he strips himself out of his giraffe suit and tries not to stare at Oskar, who has his back turned as he slips his white sleep T-shirt over his head.

Erik doesn't want sleep T-shirts. He wants naked. Fuck, he wants Oskar naked forever, preferably back in Oskar's room, with total privacy from all the ears around them, in that epic bed where Erik has pretty much decided he is going to live from now on.

Instead, he has Oskar in his sleepwear standing in the middle of the room, toothbrush in hand like this is their new routine.

The unmade bed under the roof window looks damn inviting, and Erik half contemplates tackling Oskar onto the bed and demanding that Oskar grab his first kiss so they can get on to the good bits. Like, *right now*.

But he is a decent human being, so he pulls his T-shirt on, leaves his boxers in place and follows Oskar out into the hallway, the floor of which is littered with children tucked up in sleeping bags. Emilia is fast asleep, curled up like a little worm in between the older boys, who are playing on their handheld gaming consoles while chatting excitedly. They've had a good day, Erik thinks as he steps over their legs to get into the bathroom, closing the door behind him.

The bathroom light is too harsh on his eyes, and he blinks helplessly as he wets his toothbrush and starts brushing, while Oskar just stands there watching him, his head cocked to the side.

He's beautiful. He doesn't even have to try. He can just stand there in the bright bathroom light with his threadbare T-shirt and look like he should be painted onto murals and have sonnets written about him.

"What's on your mind?" Erik asks with a smile. He wipes his mouth on the towel and hangs it back on the hook. Because he is a good kid. His mum trained him well.

That thought goes down the plughole when Oskar tackles him against the wall, and...*God.*

God help me.

Oskar's lips press against Erik's, and he can't breathe with *all this Oskar* plastered over him. He is being kissed—well, kind of sledgehammered—into the wall, and his cock is throbbing in his boxers, and...*shit.* This is not what he planned, but he's quite happy to run with it, seeing as it's Oskar. He'll take Oskar however he comes. And if it includes getting his skull slammed into the tiled bathroom wall and his teeth knocked down his throat while Oskar's fingernails scratch the skin off his cheeks, then Erik is up for it. All in. One hundred per cent. Yup.

"Slow down, baby. I'm not going anywhere," he pants out as he walks Oskar across the floor into the shower cubicle. A little squeak comes out of Oskar's mouth as Erik tips his chin up. "Slow down," he whispers again and leans in, gently pressing his lips against Oskar's.

Much better. Although Oskar is squirming and clinging to him, and there's a knee climbing his hip and Oskar's hands seem to be everywhere at once—on his shoulder, under his T-shirt, cupping his ass—while Erik keeps his own hands firmly around Oskar's face.

There's also the embarrassing fact that he's now dry-humping Oskar's stomach, jerking his hips against the poor guy, who is now the one being pressed into the wall.

This is absolutely not what Erik planned. He needs to slow down. Start again. Or he would if he could just gather enough strength to stop his tongue from licking Oskar's lips. That would have been something.

Oskar growls and his hands land firmly on Erik's chest, shoving him into the wall on the other side of the shower cubicle.

"*Shit!*" Oskar hisses as the water suddenly pours down on them, and Erik can't help himself. He bursts out laughing.

❄

Oskar wants to die. Well, no. He doesn't. Because Erik is right where he needs him, scooping him up in his arms with a smile on his face, and there's that comforting, familiar touch of warm palms all over Oskar's back. Erik is right here with him, both their T-shirts drenched and clinging to them under the lukewarm shower spray which infuriatingly seems to be washing away all of Oskar's bravery.

"Told you I don't know what I am doing," he mutters, hiding in Erik's neck. "I need lessons."

"You are bloody perfect," Erik whispers back, then kisses him, and Oskar is somehow firing on all cylinders again. His cock stirs back to life, and he becomes aware of Erik's erection poking his stomach. Oskar did that. He turns Erik on. His chest puffs up with pride at the thought that this is actually happening.

A tongue pushes between his lips, and then they are kissing —*with tongues!*—while Oskar's sad excuse for a tongue awkwardly flops around taking it all in. His senses are kind of overwhelmed by the softness and wetness and warmth in his mouth, their tangled breaths, those freaky little moans that come from him unbidden as he tries to keep his lips latched to Erik's while water streams down their faces like they're caught in an early spring shower.

"Too cold." Erik shivers and lets go of Oskar's face. The water becomes warmer, folding around Oskar like a blanket, and then Erik is back, grinding against him, and there is this delicious friction against his cock as Erik slides up. Oskar tips his head back and…*oh fuck*, Erik's lips kiss down his jaw, down his neck…*oh. Oh.*

Oh!

"Don't stop. Please don't stop," Oskar whispers. *Please.* Because he wants to go all the way. He wants this to last forever, or at least until he comes. *Please let me come. Please just keep doing what you're doing.*

Erik lightly nips at Oskar's trapezius muscle. Well, there's some wet fabric between his skin and Erik's lips, but not for long, as Erik yanks the T-shirt over Oskar's head, and then he's back, planting soft kisses that make Oskar's breath hitch, and he's making those noises again. Crazy little squeals escaping from his mouth as Erik moves on to his pectoralis major, nuzzling his nose against Oskar's nipple. *Fuck. Go back up.*

Of course, Erik does. Because he's a freaking mindreading superhero and knows exactly what Oskar wants, and now Oskar is rutting desperately against Erik as his nipple is bombarded with alternating licks and kisses, and *fuck!* Oskar is going to come. He couldn't stop it if he tried.

He tries to focus, mapping out the muscles under his skin like he's reading from one of his textbooks or the flash cards he's created in colourful marker pen. *Serratus, external oblique, rectus abdominis…* Oskar names the muscles in his groin as Erik kisses his way down there, but his mind isn't working anymore. It's fuzzy and blank and painful…and wonderful and bloody amazing.

That's Erik's mouth. Nuzzling right where Oskar's cock is being strangled by the wet fabric, *and fuck. Those are my hands. Yep.* Oskar tangles his fingers in Erik's hair, pushing and tugging to keep Erik right where he needs him as he totally loses control.

There are kids outside the door. There are people downstairs. There's a boy with his face in Oskar's groin, but Oskar doesn't care anymore. He shoots his seed into his sodden underpants that are clinging to his hips. His hips which won't stop moving, and his whole body is shaking, his head slung back against the cold tiles.

He wants to laugh out loud. How was this ever a good idea? How is this happening to him?

He's made a complete fool of himself again, he's sure, as he sinks down next to Erik, who is leaning to the side, still on his knees under the warm spray.

Erik, who has his eyes closed, snuffling uncomfortably with his hand in his boxers, little erratic tugs of his hand and desperate moans spilling from his lips as Oskar loses control again.

He shouldn't do things like this. He should think. Stop himself. Know better.

Instead, he swats Erik's hand out of the way and replaces it with his own inside the clingy fabric, gripping the warm, hard cock that pulses in his grip.

It takes nothing, not even a tug, before Erik's face is against Oskar's shoulder, silently screaming into his skin as Oskar's hand is coated with come and water and warmth, and fuck, he can feel his own cock jerk at the sensations of it all.

They don't need to speak. It's just…

Oskar came in his pants. In Erik's face. Then he jerked Erik off. He thinks. Well, he's still sitting here with Erik's cock in his hand, and his other hand is tangled in Erik's hair, so the evidence speaks for itself, and Erik, *fuck*. Erik is this amazing human being who is sniffling and almost sobbing into Oskar's chest, and Oskar finally understands. *This* is what it's all about. This all-consuming warmth falling around them like an aura of calm, which in reality, is the water from the shower, but fuck that. This is love. This is what it feels like to love and be loved—when you drop all the shields and pretence of being all nice and polite and perfect. In the end, it's just carnal instinct and pleasure and being human.

They made each other come, and it was amazing. And now they are here, and strangely, this is fine. It's more than fine.

"Let's clean up and get into bed, baby." He's just called Erik baby. *Oops!* He kind of promised himself he'd never go down the route of terms of endearment. He's far too sensible for that. His mouth apparently disagrees because it says it again.

"Baby. Come on. Stand up. Let's get these clothes off and get you warm and dry, and then we can go snuggle in bed."

"I love you," Erik snuffles. "I love you so much."

"Love you too." Oskar smiles and presses another kiss onto the lips in front of him.

Kissing. Wow. Who'd have thought? There will be more of that, he hopes. Lots more.

TWENTY-ONE

25th December

Tap. Tap, tap, tap.

Oskar wakes up with a jerk and swings his legs over the side of the bed in automatic mode, looking around in confusion. He has no clue where he is. He scratches his head and yawns. *Oh, yes. Of course.*

Erik's dad laughs and places the steaming-hot cup on the side next to him. "This will wake you up, and just remember—the good stuff will be waiting for us when we come back. The naughty stuff." He chuckles again and retreats towards the door, which is when Oskar realises he is stark naked.

In front of Erik's dad.

Oh, shit.

Einar closes the door behind him, leaving Oskar sitting on the edge of the bed with his legs crossed in embarrassment. Not that Erik's dad would have seen much since the room is dark, but even so…

Ugh. Will life never stop taunting him?

He leans back against Erik, who is asleep behind him. His Erik. Soft, lovely Erik who lets him do as much kissing as he wants.

Oskar grins like a loon because he loves Erik, and Erik loves him and loves his body and keeps touching him all over and makes him feel all mushy and loved and excited.

They stayed awake for ages last night, tangled up in each other under the duvet, kissing and cuddling and talking about all kinds of stupid things—things that made Oskar insanely happy.

They talked about kissing. Boys and girls. Crushes and people and school. They talked about growing up. Growing old. Family. About all their hopes and dreams.

✻

Oskar has always wanted to be a dad, but not like his dad. No, he wants to be the kind of father who does stuff with his kid, plays football and walks in the mountains and turns life into an adventure. But he wants to be a bit like his own dad too. Successful and respected and pretty damn cool. Oskar's dad dresses well, in smart suits with his hair gelled back, but when he is off duty, it's all about hoodies and beanies and sharp parka coats.

Oskar wants to dress like that. He just doesn't know how to put things together and look cool. Not like Erik, who is effortlessly hip whatever he wears. None of that matters, though, because Erik wants kids too. He wants babies, and he wants to adopt, and he wants to foster and make a difference to some kid's life. Listening to Erik, Oskar lay there smiling and falling in love all over again with the bizarre boy draped naked against his chest. He makes it so easy to believe in that future that Erik so easily paints for the two of them.

A future with this popular boy who looks like a million-dollar movie star, despite the patches of acne on his face and the small constellations of birthmarks on his neck. Oskar can't quite make his thoughts make sense anymore. It's unreal.

It's also pretty painful to put on his running gear this morning, especially as he would much rather curl up with his head on Erik's chest and wake him up with kisses. Today, he's going to be brave and ask about blow jobs. Yes, he wants one, but he wants to learn how to give one too. Surely, Erik will know how to give good head— Oskar once overheard someone saying she had blown Erik at some party. He'll just ask for some pointers, some helpful hints on where to start.

Dammit. Now he has a semi-boner in his spandex pants, and he gets up awkwardly, spilling some of the hot lemon and ginger down his front.

Pulling his hat over his head, he closes Erik's bedroom door behind him and manages to gulp the last of the hot liquid on his way downstairs, where he leaves the cup in the sink before heading out into the dark morning.

It's really dark. And really bloody cold, the hard snow crunching under his feet as he walks down the drive to where Einar stands on his skis waiting.

"Look over there, under the streetlight," he whispers and points. Oskar looks. There's a fox digging in the snow. It's an adult, but it's almost like the animal is playing—jumping and scratching at the snow to get to whatever is hiding underneath.

"I love seeing all the wildlife out here," Oskar whispers. "The only thing I come across running in Oslo is people. And a few birds."

"I know. I love it here. Lots of wildlife, and hardly any people around. Are you ready? Do you need to warm up before we hit full speed?" Einar gives him an evil grin, the same as his son's. Eyes twinkling and that smirk that says he's going to run Oskar fast and hard. Have him sprinting through the icy patches like his arse is on fire while Einar glides effortlessly along the tracks.

"Nope. Bring it on," Oskar says and sets off, getting a few paces ahead before Einar overtakes him.

He smiles. This is just what he needs.

The rest of the day passes too fast, the hours disappearing in the blink of an eye. They manage a nice long, leisurely Stealth Coffee Club session in the garage, eat slow-cooked Christmas porridge for lunch, after which Oskar is beaten at yet another over-complicated board game and gets the worst sugar rush from having eaten too much of the crisp almond cake that dominated the table. In the afternoon, they have an epic gingerbread baking session before Erik reminds him that they have seats on the six o'clock train, and if they're going to catch it, they'll need to bribe someone to drive them to the station.

Oskar stands in his cat onesie, in the middle of the living room with a gingerbread biscuit dangling from his mouth and Lottie on his hip, and he feels like someone has punched him in the stomach.

He is not ready to go home. He is so not ready. He wants to stay.

Stay in this warm bubble of love and laughter and safety and peaceful chaos.

But he knows he can't.

With a sombre nod, he hands Lottie back to her mum, goes and gets changed and packs his bag.

He hardly brought anything, but he folds his onesie up and strokes the fabric as he places it in his bag and tugs the zip shut. Next, he goes down and gets his decoration from the tree, because he wants to take that home too. It's his, after all, and he will forever treasure it. Take it out and look at it whenever life is getting him down. And if he ever he feels sad, he's confident that just getting into his cat onesie will bring him back here, to this place where his mind is at peace and life is simple.

He walks back downstairs like a doomed man on the way to the gallows, head hanging low. He doesn't want to go.

Leila takes his bag from him and unzips it, and for one awful moment, he thinks she's taking back his onesie, but she doesn't. She loads him up with plastic containers of food and biscuits and cakes and a bottle of julebrus—in case they need some cheer on that dreadfully boring train ride, she says. Then she holds up the box of wrapped sweets that she won in her own 'Coin in the Gingerbread Loaf competition' and gives Oskar a smile and a wink as she tips the contents into his bag.

He wants to cry. Throw himself on the floor like the kid who doesn't want to leave the party. Instead, he revels in getting one last session of love therapy. He no longer minds the hugs or the cringeworthy sentiments Erik's mum whispers in his ear. He needs them. He is important. He is loved. He is so very, very much loved.

Oddly, he kind of knows he is, and it's messing with his head.

❄

At least this time they have seats. The train has barely started to move when they have to stop waving at Elise and Geir, who drove them to the station. Oskar feels empty and more than a little numb.

"These past days have felt like living in this bubble. Like the life I lead in Oslo is so far removed from reality, I just can't grasp it."

"I know," Erik whispers. "It's been the best Christmas. I love going home. We can go again whenever you want to. Just pop home for the weekend to chill out. I know Mum and Dad would love to see you again, and you need to cuddle Lottie, and Emilia loves you, and even Linus told me that you're a really cool dude. I need to bring Linus up to Oslo next year and take him to a concert or something. Emmy did that with me when I was sixteen—took me to see Bon Jovi at the Spectrum—and I remember thinking it was the most amazing experience. We need to plan, come up with a band we want to see, and we can book it and bring him as a surprise. Something cool."

It's a bit much for Oskar's brain to take in. All these plans for the future when he can't even grasp what's going to happen within the next hour.

Rather than worry about that, he buries his face in Erik's chest, and Erik holds him, rocking him gently with his fingers tangling in Oskar's hair as he jabbers on about concerts and artists and the epic New Year's party the boys upstairs are in charge of. Luckily, the party venue is *not* upstairs. No, this time they have the full use of the campus cafeteria and community centre, sponsorship from a local craft brewery, food courtesy of the catering college, and some local celebrity known from TV is coming to DJ, meaning that the whole thing will be mind-blowingly epic.

Oskar is not going anywhere near it, however epic it may be.

He's going to stay at home, like he always does, and probably have a panic attack about Erik not coming back to sleep in his bed. He doesn't care if Erik is drunk as a skunk as long as his skinny arse ends up back in Oskar's bed. He wants to tell him that, but he thinks it might be creepy to demand that after being Erik's boyfriend for what? Two days?

They may be boyfriends and kiss and be all super-snuggly cuddly like they are now, but Oskar doesn't know the rules, and he doesn't want to be that kind of person. Someone like his mum, full of questions and demands and timings and ultimatums. That's just not him.

But he needs to start somewhere, and he needs to know where he stands.

"Baby, what happens when we get back home? What happens to us? To this?" Oskar lifts his head to meet Erik's eyes.

Erik looks like he wants to cry. The words spill out of his mouth, almost like he can't stop himself. "I don't know."

It's such a shit, clichéd thing to say. They're not even back in Oslo yet, but Erik is already morphing back to his old self, and it hurts. Oskar of all people should know better than to think this whole fairy-tale would last. But then Erik loves Oskar, he said so. He said he loves Oskar so much it's a little bit frightening. It's not fair. All of this is not fair at all.

But then Erik was just being honest. This Christmas had been brilliant, the absolute best ever, and Oskar wants to scream as the truth hits him, because this was always the inevitable aftermath. This Christmas fling they'd had, or whatever it was, was probably all it would ever be, and now it was time to face the facts and get back to reality.

Shit.

TWENTY-TWO

They walk hand in hand, leaving the Central station like they belong together. Because they do. Erik knows that. Oskar makes him insanely happy, but people talk, and there will be gossip. Words that will not always be kind.

He can take it. Hell, he's sometimes done it himself—thrown out careless comments for a few seconds of laughter. He deserves whatever people choose to throw back at him, but it's time he stood up for himself and owned it.

He is gay. Fine.

He has a boyfriend. Super fine.

He needs to start being honest and telling people that. Not fine.

Fucking scary.

The most frightening thing of all is that he knows Oskar doesn't want this. He doesn't want people to know his business, and Erik can understand that. Still, Erik has no intention of *not* sleeping in Oskar's bed every night. He intends to do a lot of stuff in Oskar's bed. Which reminds him… They need to stop at a convenience store and buy a few essential things.

"We need to buy condoms," he blurts out as they walk down a nice, normal residential street.

Oskar almost trips over his feet. "Okay," he replies, smiling nervously.

"And lube. We'll need lube. Not that I am saying that we have to do all these things right now, but we might want to. One day. Eventually. And we'll need to have these things. Better be prepared." Erik needs to shut up before Oskar runs away and never speaks to him again, but Erik doesn't have any condoms because he hasn't had the urge to go that far with anyone for a long, long time, and if they don't stop somewhere now—

"I want a blow job." Oskar almost vomits the words, his breath steaming out in front of him. "I've never had one, and I want to at least know what it's like." He can't even look at Erik, but this is good. They're talking about things. Important things.

"You can have as many blow jobs as you want. I can't guarantee I'll be any good at them, but I'll try. And you need to tell me what you like. What feels good."

Oskar shakes his head. "I can't believe we're walking across my old schoolyard talking about blow jobs."

"You went here, to this school?" Erik stops and looks up the ornate brick buildings looming over them, the shiver-inducing deserted, dark windows, the icy benches dotted along the edges of the open square. "Wow! Cool school!"

"I hated it. Spent most of my time hiding from idiots and trying to pass all my exams so I could get out of here."

Oskar looks so sad, and Erik can't stand it. He wraps him up in a hug. Kisses his cheeks. Kisses his lips. Little, soft, comforting kisses.

"I wish I'd been here to look after you. I'd have protected you. Sat with you and brought you coffee and held your hand. I wish I'd met you years ago. Then I wouldn't have made so many mistakes and hurt people."

"Why? Who have you hurt?" Oskar studies him, all honest and kind and wonderful, and Erik thinks he might start to cry again. He has never cried this much over being happy in his life. It's pretty stupid, to be honest.

"Mostly girls I messed around with. I wanted to be normal. I wanted to be like everyone else—kissing and making out and having sex and being this cool bloke. I hurt a few people just by being an arsehole, acting the fool. I was fake when I should have been honest, making fun of other people so nobody would see through all my lies. But I always messed up in the end and then I'd get drunk and...I'm not always a good person, Oskar. I don't want to be like that anymore. I want to be honest about who I am. I want to be happy, but I don't know how to make the old me become the new me. I don't know how to be me anymore."

"Hey." Oskar tightens his arms around Erik. "I just want to be with *you*. Let's just see how things work out. Whatever happens, I love you. I mean that, because…Well, I do. I've never been in love before, so I don't know what I'm supposed to do and say, but…"

Erik is crying again—just a tear or two—because it's so damn comforting not being alone. Being honest. Being brave. Standing here with Oskar in a deserted schoolyard on a frosty December evening where everything suddenly seems so clear and easy.

"You know that night after the party?" Oskar kisses the tears away. "When you ended up in my bed?"

"Yeah?"

"That wasn't just a drunken mistake, was it?" Oskar's smiling as he asks, his eyes sparkling in the glow from the streetlights.

"No," Erik admits, leaning into Oskar's gloved hand as it cups his cheek. "I was so tired. Tired and sad and lonely, in a room full of people having a good time. I just wanted to feel something, and I didn't even care if you laughed in my face or punched me, or if you never spoke to me again. So I went downstairs to find you and tell you I was in love with you and would do anything to be with you. That's how piss drunk and pathetic I was. But you weren't there. Your room was empty, so I guess I must have just curled up in your bed thinking I'd wait for you. I don't really remember anything after that. Sorry."

Oskar laughs. "You silly, silly boy." Kisses his eyelids. His cheeks. His lips. "I'm happy you came to me. I'm so happy you came."

"Me too." Erik sniffles and flashes a little smile. "Best thing I ever did. And I couldn't believe how cute you were when I woke up. You were all angry and tense and feisty, and all I wanted to do was give you a hug. God, it was a fucked-up morning, wasn't it?"

"Mmm. It was the weirdest morning of my life. But also the best morning of my life." Oskar does the nose rub again, and his eyes twinkle mischievously.

"Why was that?" Erik asks, grabbing Oskar's hand as they set off again across the yard towards the road.

"Because I realised that I didn't want to be alone anymore, and how nice it was to have someone there, you know? And somehow, you didn't scare me. Well, you did at first, but once you started talking and being all grumpy and funny, I decided I liked you. That you were safe. It was nice. Really nice."

❄

They walk in silence the rest of the way, letting their arms swing between them, gloved hands laced in a firm grip, sharing little glances now and then, smiles and nudges. Erik seems lost in thought, and Oskar…

He can't bear it. All the anxieties are returning, brewing inside him like angry moths, flapping and taunting him when he should be happy and calm. He has nothing to worry about. Yet he has everything to worry about—all these little simple things that could so easily tip his world off its new, fragile axis.

"Come sleep with me," Oskar blurts out as Erik pulls off his glove with his teeth to punch in the code that opens the front door to the dorm block.

"Of course I will. Why on earth would I sleep anywhere else?" Erik looks hurt, like he can't believe Oskar had to ask.

"Good," Oskar says. It is good. Isn't it?

"You're worrying again. Oskar, please don't be worried. I'll sneak out before anyone wakes up, and I'll try not to make your life more complicated. I just need to be with you."

Fucking hell. Oskar doesn't know how Erik does it. How he just stands there and looks at him, his face all open and honest, and how his mouth churns out all these perfect words that make Oskar feel all warm on the inside.

"I don't want you to sneak out. I want to wake up with you in the morning. I don't think I care what anyone thinks anymore. It's not important. They can gossip and tease me all they want, I really don't care." Oskar laughs and shrugs his shoulders. He honestly wouldn't care if the two of them walked in holding hands right now and were seen by the entire dorm. He needs to own this. He needs be brave and honest and figure this out, once and for all. For himself. For Erik.

"You want to be out in the open about us?" Erik looks a little surprised and Oskar shrugs again.

"I don't want to go back to the way things were. Things need to be different now, because I have you. Don't I?"

He doesn't know why he feels the need to question it. Erik is his. Erik, who cries at a drop of a hat, who smiles so easily and lets Oskar kiss him and sleeps naked next to him. Erik, whose hands are around Oskar's face, holding him steady as they kiss again and Oskar melts. Squeaks a little in delight at the tongue action and kind of…tries to…

He seriously needs to figure out what to do with his tongue because he's quite sure he's never seen people kiss as sloppily as he does. All lips and spit and…ugh. It's still amazing, though, however uncoordinated and un-movie-like their little make-out sessions end up.

I have nothing to lose. Nothing. He can't think of anything worse than going back to his old life, of being alone and tired. He doesn't recall ever feeling lonely, but he must have been because the sheer thought of not having Erik next to him has him breaking out in an angst-ridden sweat.

"Promise me," he breathes and presses his lips to Erik's. A little desperately, perhaps, but right now, he is fucking desperate. "Promise me we fix this. That we make this work. Promise me things will be okay, Erik, because I need this. I need you to help me fix this."

"Fix what, baby?" Erik frowns, confused. "Nothing's broken. We're not broken, are we?"

"No." Oskar smiles a little bit. He's being absurd. "We're not broken. I just don't know how to do this. How to be us."

"I don't know how to be us either, but we'll have a lot of fun figuring it out, won't we? I'm going to stick with you forever. Get used to it."

He pushes the door open, and Oskar kind of gets half carried over the doorstep, clinging to Erik with his lips latched onto that luscious mouth of his. He doesn't even let go when he sticks his key into the door of 212:A, still far too lost in messily kissing Erik and sucking on his tongue and bashing teeth against teeth and giggling softly when…

There's water all over the floor, flowing in a steady stream from the kitchen area. Oskar has never seen so much of it, and it's *everywhere*. He lets go of Erik and runs towards the kitchen.

She's on the floor, sodden from head to toe, shivering in her wet clothes while bleachy water pools around her. She's not even attempting to scrub and seems barely aware of her surroundings.

"Naomi, sweetheart. Oh, fucking hell, Naomi." Oskar sinks to his knees at her side. He has no idea if he should touch her or not, how to ground her—how to make her look at him.

"I needed you and you weren't here," she whispers. "It was all too much, and I couldn't cope, so I came home because you would be here to make it better, and you weren't here."

Oskar looks over at Erik, thinking, *just go*.

Then thinking, *no, please don't go. Don't leave me. Please help me because this is so out of hand. Be everything I need you to be right now. I can't do this on my own anymore. Please. Just be you because when you are you, I am fine. When you are you, I can be me and we can fix this. We can fix the whole fucking world when we are together. I know we can. So. Please.*

And Erik…

Erik looks at him. Looks right back at him with all that love in his eyes.

"I'm getting help," he says. "We need help."

TWENTY-THREE

She's broken and it's bad. Oskar has seen Naomi in every kind of state. She can be happy and lively and insanely snarky and funny and sarcastic and flirty. She can also be lost, so far away in her head that he thinks she'll never find her way back into the real world, her eyes glazed over and dead, her body limp as he almost drags her along the corridor towards her room.

He needs to switch off this water, he thinks, but he files it away for later. He can mop water all night, that doesn't matter. Right now, Naomi needs calm. She needs help. She needs *him*.

It's something he's thought about before, long before he met Naomi. When someone needs him, he can direct all his focus on that and forget about everything else clouding his brain. He functions well when he is needed. And he thinks maybe he should go into emergency medicine because he can cope with this—rash decisions and quick plans and pushing the non-important things to the back of his mind.

He doesn't even think about what he's doing as he switches on the shower in Naomi's bathroom and checks the temperature is nice and warm before turning around and starting to remove her clothes.

Her head is bowed, her eyes closed. She's still too weak to protest as he unbuttons her blouse and gently pulls the thin fabric over her shoulders.

She's also too thin, her skin prickled with chills. He needs to check her diet, try to get some more food into her. He needs to go shopping with her and talk about fats and carbohydrates and good oils. He almost laughs at the irony of him teaching her about good diets when he consistently burns more calories than he eats. Not that it's been a problem over Christmas, but he's such a hypocrite, lecturing Naomi in his head when his own diet is frankly shocking.

"Turn around, sweetie," he says as he pulls down her trousers, and she steps out of the wet clothes pooling around her feet, crossing her arms over her chest as he unfastens her bra and lets it fall to the floor. "There we go. You're doing great, Naomi."

"Don't leave me," she whispers.

"Not leaving. I'm right here, and we're going to fix everything. Come on—get in the shower and get warm. I'm going to go and turn the water off, then I'll sit with you, okay? Everything's fine. Just get warm."

He has to push her under the spray of water, leaving her underpants in place. It doesn't matter, even though they've done this often enough to be well beyond a bit of awkward nudity. He's seen Naomi at her worst, and while he might be wearing clothes, with her, he is bare and honest. No anxieties. No worries. No pretending. He is always himself with Naomi.

He pulls the shower curtain around her and kicks the wet clothes aside with his foot. He's soaked himself, but there are things that need to be done.

He jogs down the corridor to the kitchen, only to stop dead in his tracks.

The kitchen is a lot more crowded than when he left it. There are a bunch of dudes there, in hoodies and sweatpants, most of them armed with buckets, and a dude Oskar kind of knows—Hassan from his year—arrives with a pile of towels. He gives one to Oskar and nods his head.

"Disney Prince. Merry Christmas, dude."

"Uh, Merry Christmas," Oskar says awkwardly.

"Ammar!" Erik calls. "I'll start pushing the water down the corridor. If we can get it out the front door, it'll save us having to mop it up." Erik passes a mop to the dude who is apparently called Ammar—a tall, slick guy with swept-back hair who smiles at Oskar and reaches out his hand.

"Hi. Ammar. You're Oskar?" he asks like it's fine. Like this is completely chill.

"Oskar," he confirms with a calm nod, though his body is on fire, screaming *RED ALERT! RED ALERT!* and his muscles appear to be paralysed. He can't do anything but stand there like an idiot.

"Mikael and Adam are upstairs heating up food for us all, then they'll be down to help too," Erik tells him. "And I just woke up Carlos. He's going to get dressed and bring us more towels. Mathias and I will mop like crazy until Jakob comes back—he's gone to find more buckets. There are some in the laundry block, and rags, so we'll have this cleaned up in no time. You're out of cleaning stuff, by the way. I think she tipped it all out, so we'll have to pick up more tomorrow. No problem." Erik shrugs and looks at Oskar, like he's expecting a reply.

Oskar can't say a thing, not with all these people here. Not when Erik looks amazing—all handsome and cool with his hair slicked back and his hoodie slung around his waist and his head held high, like he is the king of everything. Not while all these dudes are staring at him waiting for him to speak. Not when everyone is expecting Oskar to be something he is definitely not.

So, he just nods weakly and turns around. Walks briskly back to Naomi's door. A heavy hand hits his shoulder.

"What?" he snarls. He hasn't got a clue what he's doing right now. He's not safe.

"How is she?"

The boy who asks—okay, he's not a boy. He's tall and wide, and his floppy fringe is all over his face. He pushes it back to reveal eyes so dark and full of worry that Oskar instantly calms down. A tiny bit.

"Bad," he says. "And you are?"

"Victor." The dude grabs Oskar's hand and shakes it vigorously. "Can I help? Please tell me what I can do. I can't stand here and do nothing when she's hurting."

Oskar wants to laugh. What does this guy know about hurting? What the hell does he know about having a hard life? How can he possibly understand anything about the world being a black hole with no way of crawling back up into the light? This guy doesn't know shit.

But if Christmas with Erik has taught Oskar one thing, it's to not judge a book by its very jock-like cover, so he pushes the laughter aside and asks, "Can you see if you can find her some pyjamas? Something warm and soft and comforting. Something she'll feel safe in?"

Victor nods and steps past Oskar, kicking off his shoes in the small hallway before opening Naomi's wardrobe.

She's still in the shower, and Oskar switches off the water, then unfolds one of the towels from the neat stack, holding it open, arms wide. Naomi steps into his embrace, and he relaxes as he folds his arms around her, moves the soft towelling over her back in firm movements, trying to calm himself as much as it seems to soothe her. She's breathing better now. Strong, steady breaths against his chest, not the erratic huffs she was letting out earlier.

"I'm going to get some clothes on you now, okay?" He keeps his voice low, confident but quiet. He's in control. She only has to follow. No need to think. "Just shut off your brain and rest. Heal. It will be fine."

This Victor dude is solid, he thinks as an arm reaches through the bathroom door to deposit a bunch of clothing. A soft cotton vest, a fleece top, brushed pyjama pants and bed socks. Soft and warm and comforting to the soul.

Oskar almost giggles as he realises. He has *definitely* spent too much time with Erik's mum, and now his hands are around Naomi's face, and he can't help but smile as she looks back at him.

"You are loved," he says before he can stop himself. "You are so much loved. Go lie down and rest now. Tomorrow is a new day. Everything will be fine."

She nods. Nods and closes her eyes again.

She is. She is loved. Because Oskar has realised some truths this Christmas, learned some interesting facts. Like that he has friends. He has people who love him, and he is not alone, not by any measure. It might just be words, a random hug from an excited child, a baby squealing while pulling his hair, but he is loved, and it feels so very, very good.

"Naomi, this is Victor," he says as he leads her into her room, and Oskar really thinks this dude is pretty awesome now, because Victor has made up her bed, pulled back the covers and drawn the curtains closed. The bedside light is on low, and he sits on the floor flipping through one of the books she keeps neatly stacked by her desk. "Victor's safe, I promise."

Well, Oskar doesn't know Victor, who might be a total psycho and more fucked up in the head than he seems, but Erik said he likes Naomi. Erik said he's a good guy, and in Oskar's book, that will do. There's so much going on in his head right now that he thinks Erik has probably saved the day again. Oskar needs help, so he grabs it.

"Victor, can you sit with Naomi for a bit while I go and get dry and change?"

Victor nods, and Oskar folds the duvet over Naomi, who has curled into the foetal position on the bed, her arms tight around her knees.

"Don't touch her without asking her if it's okay first. She doesn't like to be touched without permission by people she doesn't know. Just talk to her, tell her something. Keep her calm." Oskar is doing his pseudo-doctor thing again, but Victor doesn't seem to mind.

"Hi, Naomi. I'm Victor. Is it all right that I am here?" He looks concerned. His voice at the right pitch, and Oskar wonders if he's a medical student too. He's actually never paid enough attention to the guys upstairs to recognise who they are or if he already knows them. Oskar's beginning to think he might be a bit of an arsehole himself, somewhere deep down.

By the time he's cleaned up Naomi's shower, put her clothes in her laundry basket and hung the towel on the hook on the wall, he finds Victor holding her hand, his thumb moving gently over her broken skin as he reads to her from the book in his other hand, his voice low and soothing.

Something in Oskar breaks a little, because this—maybe this is something that could be good, yet a tiny part of him is angry, fuelled by some irrational jealousy. This should be his job. This is *his* place, on the floor with Naomi's hand in his. This is what he does. Sits there and soothes her until she is asleep and calm. He has even, on occasion, dozed off with his head against the mattress, his hand never leaving hers.

He no longer belongs here and is still a bit murky on where he does belong. He needs to go and be with Erik. He needs a hug and to find out if *this* Erik—the cool, tall, strait-laced dude out there in the corridor, shouting commands to the other guys roaming around the common room of 212:A— is still *his* Erik.

He needs to tell them to be quiet, and not upset Naomi any further. Except her face is calm, her eyes closed, her head relaxed against the pillow in the soft light. This could be just what she needs —someone who can be everything to her that Oskar can never be.

He leaves, closing the door gently behind him.

TWENTY-FOUR

Oskar slips into his room unnoticed, hiding away like he always does. He's always been the master of making himself invisible.

It's like nothing has changed, like he's still sixteen hiding from everyone at school, frightened and jumpy. Scared of his own shadow. He's not brave anymore. He is nobody. Nothing. Himself.

His clothes are in a pile on the floor, and he kicks them angrily into the wall as he stomps into the shower. He hadn't noticed how cold he is until now, wet from the damp clothes and probably a little bit exhausted. It's been a weird day. It feels like light years ago that he woke up in Erik's bed and went running and had coffee, and he can't even remember all the other stuff they've done today.

He hasn't eaten for a while either, his body weak and still shivering under the warm spray, and he's pissed off. He knew this would end badly. He knew this was a fucking stupid idea, and *still* he fell for the whole fairy tale that this could be his life.

Of course it can't.

Because Oskar Høiland is just who he is. An insecure freaking loser.

He was fine an hour ago.

Now? He is not so fine now, he thinks, as he slams the handle for the shower against the wall and rubs the towel a little too vigorously against his head, the hard fabric scratching against his skin until it's red and angry.

Fucking, fucking, fucking, *shit!*

He wants to go out there and steal Erik back. Get them both on a train and go back to Moss.

Fuck, he might just go on his own. He'd do anything to crawl back into the safety of Erik's bed with the squeaky bedframe and the thin mattress and the Star Wars covers that scream *safety* and *love* and *home* to him.

But he can't. Instead, he pulls on a tracksuit and some mismatched socks and hopes there's still some power left in his laptop, because he can't for the life of him remember where he last saw the charger.

He wants to scream. Shout. Cry. Curl up in a ball like Naomi and rock himself into a stupor.

Erik loves me. I love Erik. It doesn't make any sense right now, almost like he imagined it all. Made it up in his head and it's just some stupid daydream. It's too much. Too much for his body to take. Too much pain and rejection and disappointment and anger, and all these feelings he can't deal with. His body just can't deal with anything right now, and he sinks, every muscle going slack as he tumbles onto the bed, headfirst, his whole body collapsing, one cell at a time.

"Hey." Erik's here, crawling up the bed, his arms curling around Oskar's body. Oskar didn't even clock the door opening or the soft click as it closed again. "Baby?" Erik says, and Oskar wants to cry. Fuck. He thought he was getting good at this love thing, but he is obviously totally crap at it.

Erik is all around him, legs over his legs, arms around his body, his face in his neck. His lips kiss and nuzzle, and Oskar's tears are stupid. Freaking stupid. This strange body of his that he has no control over anymore.

"I love you. I love you, and I don't know how to do this," Oskar cries, but Erik just smiles against his cheek.

"I love you too. Come on, the food's ready outside. Mikael's mum sent down so many treats for us. She makes these amazing flatbreads, and there are lamb koftas and chicken stew—it smells divine. You eat it all with your hands with this white garlic sauce, and it's just amazing. Don't let Adam trick you into trying his chillies, though. They're Mauritian pickled chillies—tiny little things that look all cute and innocent and then blow your tongue out of your mouth. Trust me. Say no to the chillies."

"I don't know," Oskar says. He's such a coward. He's supposed to be a grown-up, and here he is being terrified of a bunch of perfectly normal students.

"Don't be scared," Erik murmurs, "I'll be right next to you. Everyone's shattered, and it's been a long day. We just need to eat, and then we are coming back here, back to this bed. Oh, and Carlos was with some girl—he made her come down too, and she looks even more terrified than you do. He's usually really shy with the girls, but I think he likes this one. Come on," Erik coaxes, "you can help talk to her down before she faints."

Oskar turns around, wriggles until he's face-to-face with Erik and places a tiny little kiss on the tip of his nose.

"Kissing lesson number one," Erik whispers. "Kisses go on the lips. On my lips. Okay?"

"Not on your nose?" Oskar teases playfully. The bubbles in his veins are back. His body going all love-stupid again.

"Okay, sometimes on the nose, but right now, I need kisses on my lips. Just here." Erik points. "Your mouth on mine. Just soft, soft, soft. There…"

Oskar is a good student. Of course he is. So he kisses Erik's lips. Kisses them like he means it. Soft and sweet and *fuck*, these lessons are no good. Because there's that tongue again, and there are lips, and he is fucking starving when it comes to Erik, who tastes of love and happiness and Christmas and sugar and makes all the anger and sadness in Oskar's stomach disappear with just a press of his mouth to his.

Like magic.

He somehow ends up straddling Erik, out of breath and light-headed from kissing. From being loved. From the freaking adrenaline that shoots through his body every time Erik touches him or kisses him—hell, his body goes into meltdown as soon as they're in the same bloody room.

"What are you doing to me?" he laughs into Erik's mouth.

"Loving you," Erik whispers back.

Oskar's body likes that. He grabs a pillow and hits Erik over the head with it like he's lost his mind. He has, it's true, because he doesn't know how to deal with all this happiness. A few minutes ago, he was crying into that same pillow, and now he can't stop laughing as he hits Erik over the head with it.

Erik, who is laughing and grabbing at him and trying to wrestle him back to the mattress. Erik, who kisses him. Erik, who loves him. He loves him. It's freaking…*lovely*.

"Come eat," Erik whispers. "Then, I'll throw them all out and take you to bed and give you the best attempt of a blow job you've ever had."

"The *only* blow job I have ever had." Oskar giggles.

"First of many," Erik says, laughing too. "Is Naomi okay?"

"Victor is sitting with her. I'll go check on her in a bit."

"Good. He's so lost. He just needs someone to need him. He's one of those people who has so much to give but doesn't know how to give it. I think he'd be good for her, and she would be so good for him. If they can just talk and hang out, maybe it's a start?"

Oskar could go into a long explanation about Naomi and her needs and how another man in her life is about as good for her as a hole in the head, but Erik…is right. As always.

Erik, kisses him again and pokes a fingertip under the elastic in Oskar's joggers, and Oskar is almost feeling brave enough to rip his pants off and shove his cock down Erik's throat like some feral alpha male in a Game of Thrones episode or something.

"Come eat!" Erik begs and twangs the elastic, while Oskar's cock turns everything that comes out of Erik's mouth into some dirty promise. Yes, he will eat. Then he will get blown. Then he wants to blow Erik. Then he wants…

"Food," Oskar says. "Then sex."

"Absolutely." Erik's smile is wider than ever. "Lots of sex. Naked. In your bed."

"Epic." Oskar laughs. He is being ridiculous, but he just doesn't care anymore.

❉

Erik needs to do this.

It's selfish in a way, but fuck, if he can make a start here, in the safety of the people he kind of thinks of as family, then maybe, maybe he can make this right. Make things work for both of them.

So what if he practically drags Oskar out to the kitchen? The boy needs to eat. They both need to eat.

And if Oskar is terrified? Well, Erik is right here with him, his hand supportively on the small of Oskar's back as he pushes him around the table and introduces him to the guys, who enthusiastically shake Oskar's hand while tucking into the boxes of food on the table in front of them, all served with plastic spoons on kitchen roll.

"Classy shit, this." Mikael laughs and hands Oskar a sheet of festive-patterned kitchen roll. "Less washing up. We just stuff everything in the bin when we're done." He wipes his hands and passes Oskar a warm flatbread, while Erik shuffles nervously behind him.

"Sit, my friend," Adam says and puts his hand on Erik's shoulder. "Eat, dude. You look like you're about to pass out."

"Been a long day," Erik lies. Or at least, it has been a long day, but that's not why he's on the verge of collapse. He has to stop this fucking lying, because it makes him feel sick.

"Good Christmas then, everyone?" Carlos asks and shoves another mouthful in his mouth. "I love your mum, Mikael. She can come cook for us anytime."

Jakob says, "Remember in May when she travelled down and cooked up that big feast upstairs? She was horrified at the state of the fridge, so she went down town on the bus and bought all these ingredients and filled the freezer with little bags of rice and stews and bread. We lived like kings." He grins, and the others all nod in agreement.

"Yeah, we lived like kings for about a week," Mikael laughs, "and then we were back on noodles again. Seriously, I don't know how you all ate it so fast. But she's coming back to visit in February, she promised."

Adam watches Mikael with that smile Erik recognises and envies —the smile that tells a million stories. *I love you*, it says. *I love you and I'm so fucking proud that you're mine.* It also kind of says, *Please love me as much as I love you because without you, my life would fall apart.* So many things in one small smile. And now Erik has that, or he hopes he does. He looks over at Oskar, who is nervously picking at a piece of lamb with his fingers, then relaxing as the taste hits his tongue.

Erik can almost taste it too—the rich spices, the saltiness and chilli coming through as an afterthought—when Oskar bites into the tender meat. Erik picks up a morsel of his own and puts it in his mouth, but it kind of grows until he can barely swallow it.

"Guys?" he says. A bead of sweat rolls down his forehead. He needs to do this, get it over and done with before he loses the plot.

The table falls silent, all eyes on him. He reaches out and places his hand on Oskar's, right there on the top of the table, and meets his eyes, pleading, trying to say, *I'm sorry but please let me do this. For me. Because I need to start somewhere, and this is the only place to start. Because I love you. Please.*

"Thank you for helping. You were brilliant. Honestly. Thank you."

There are mumbles around the table. Supportive words and easy nods. They would have helped. Anytime. Of course. Always.

"I took food down for Victor and his princess girl," Jakob says. "They're fine."

Everyone nods again, looking expectantly at Erik, like he's supposed to tell them what happens next. Like he has all the answers, and he usually does. He is the ringmaster—the one with the ideas. The one who pulls the strings. They expect him to take the lead, to keep them moving. Make them laugh with his stupid, reckless stunts.

"Oskar and I are together," he says quickly. His heart is beating so fast he can barely breathe for the static whizzing in his ears. "I love him. He's my boyfriend, and I love him." There's no going back now. "He's the best thing that ever happened to me. He is kind and funny and wonderful, and he makes me happy. I just need you to know. That he's with me, and I'm with him."

"We kind of knew that," Jakob smiles, and there's no teasing in his voice.

"You've been obsessed with him for a while."

"Good on you."

"Finally."

"Yay!"

"Cool."

They're all speaking at the same time, and Erik feels a little bit dizzy. There are nods. Words of kindness. Laughter. But it is kind laughter.

"Good man," Ammar says and drags Erik up from his chair, enfolding him in a hug. "You deserve it. Be happy, dude."

"Here." Someone hands him a drink. "You look a bit pale."

Not that he knows what it is, but he takes a gulp from the glass handed to him and braces for Oskar's response. He can't look at him because he doesn't know what he will get. They didn't quite talk about this. Well, they mentioned it. Kind of. And now Erik has outed them to everyone. Just like that.

"HEEEEEYYYYYYYY!"

They all turn around to find Carolina standing behind them, with her suitcase clutched in front of her and a massive grin on her face.

"Who said you lot could party in our dorm down here? And who forgot to invite me?" She wiggles her hips and throws her coat on the floor! "Bring me food, slaves. Queen Carolina has arrived!"

Everyone laughs, the chatter and giggles filling the room, and Erik finally dares to look at Oskar, who is sitting there with the biggest smile on his face, his eyes all twinkling and proud. He looks so happy and proud and gorgeous that Erik can't stop himself. He leans over and presses his lips to Oskar's, hard and fast and it's such a mess because they're both smiling, all teeth and lips and noses pressed together.

"You're mine too," Oskar says.

❆

Oskar can't stop smiling, nor can he stop the stupid half-crying he's got going on. He loves this brave, crazy, strong, wonderful Erik, who sits there smiling as Oskar dots uncoordinated little kisses all over his face. On his lips. His cheeks. His cheekbones. Top of his eyes. He loves him.

"Oh, hell. You two? You really are fucking, aren't you?" Carolina shouts above the chatter, and everything falls quiet as all eyes are on them. And because Erik makes him feel so incredibly safe and brave, Oskar just climbs right onto Erik's lap, throws his arms around his neck and clings to his boyfriend like an over-friendly monkey.

"Hell, yes!" he says, grinning like a loon. "Of course we are."

He doesn't know how to stop now he's started. He doesn't know how he's so calm about this, with all these people sitting around the table, chatting and laughing and eating like there's nothing wrong. Like this is normal. Like this is a thing he's always done.

Maybe he was wrong all along. Maybe these guys aren't that bad. They're just humans. Pretty decent humans, as it happens. He looks down the table at the blonde one—Mathias?—giving him a friendly smile. Mathias lifts his beer can, nodding at Oskar and giving him a thumbs-up and a wink when Oskar smiles back.

He knows what he needs right now. He leans in and sniffs, inhaling the scent of Erik's hair, squeezes him and holds him, and Erik does that thing on Oskar's back with his hands. Slow, strong strokes. Oskar would purr if he could. *Stay here where it's safe. With Erik.*

"Come on. Take me to bed, baby," Erik whispers.

And Oskar nods. *This. This here. Fuck.* He laughs out loud.

What the hell just happened to his life?

"Night, guys," Erik calls to the table as he drags Oskar towards the door. "Keep it quiet and fucking clean up."

"Somewhere you boys need to be?" Hassan says, and everyone roars with laughter as Erik gives them the finger.

"Love you guys," Erik shouts back, and Oskar can't help himself.

"Night, guys!" he shouts and lets Erik drag him along the corridor, hand in hand, laughter spilling from his mouth and happiness fluttering in his stomach.

"Come on, baby, let's go get naked."

"Blow job time."

"I'm going to blow your fucking mind," Erik promises.

And Oskar thinks, *you already have, baby.*

TWENTY-FIVE

This being naked in bed is pretty cool. Oskar has never slept naked—he's never liked the bareness, never felt safe—but now it's something that feels liberating. Almost like he never wants to wear clothes again. Not when he's lying flat on his back with his legs spread, every inch of him on display for all the world to see, while Erik presses little kisses down his chest. Oskar's cock is right in the game. It throbs and fills and taps against his groin as Erik's fingers dance across his skin, trailing feather-light over his hips, dipping gently into his belly button and circling his nipples, teasing, denying him what he really wants.

Fuck! He wants.

As long as Erik touches him, he's fine. And God, he wants to touch Erik too. Not that he can reach very much right now, when his fingers are tangled in Erik's hair, pulling him closer and guiding his mouth to where Oskar needs it to be.

He said. He promised. *Ugh.*

"Tell me what you need. You need to tell me what feels good," Erik whispers.

"Jhjjjslllslskk," Oskar moans as Erik's lips brush the head of his cock, pressing soft kisses over his slit. Oskar arches his hips; there is just no way he can't. He feels like a puppet, and Erik is holding his strings. With every touch, his body does things he can't control. Like his legs, which Erik are straddling, his full weight pinning them to the mattress, yet they still jerk and kick with every flick of Erik's tongue.

Erik teases the soft, loose ring of Oskar's foreskin, then licks up and down his shaft before scattering open-mouthed kisses over his balls. The sensory overload has Oskar making all kinds of noises and spilling out words that make no sense at all.

"Do you mind if I play with your balls?" Erik asks, huffing hot breath over the taut skin. Oskar moans and nods, incapable of giving a verbal response. Erik rolls his testicles between his fingers, and Oskar mumbles out nonsense.

Well, he is definitely off his head.

Erik sucks one of Oskar's balls into his mouth and pulls a little, and Oskar isn't quite sure that's his thing, so he wiggles his hips. Which makes Erik let him go with a smile and a little pop.

"Ball play," he says with a chuckle. "You can do it to me, I kind of dig it." Then he opens his mouth and stares at Oskar, who stares back. He wants so desperately to watch, but he can't because he is about to truly embarrass himself.

He's close. It's not going to take much.

❄

He's beautiful, Erik thinks. *Craning his neck so he can see what I'm doing. Which is fucking hot.* He's grateful for the light. If the room was dark, he would miss all these amazing little things, like the blush on Oskar's chest as it rises and falls, how his mouth hangs open and his eyes flicker shut when Erik's lips close around his cock. He tastes just as he looks. Sweet, sharp and delicious.

Salty fluid spills into Erik's mouth, and there's a soft throbbing against his tongue, just like the little jerks of his own cock when he's trying to hold back. He knows this feeling—the last seconds of almost-painful pleasure before he falls over the edge and swan-dives into orgasm.

Sex was never like this before, though to be honest, Erik doesn't think he's ever had sex sober. He's also never been so hell-bent on making someone else feel good, and right now he's freaking acing it if Oskar's writhing and moans are anything to go by.

It's a heady feeling, being able to do this—making someone he loves fall apart, and to have them trust him enough that they just let go. Oskar's head is thrown back, and his eyes are closed, and Erik may need to have words about the hair pulling. He quite likes having his hair attached to his head, thank you very much, but Oskar has a thing for burying his hands in Erik's and tugging at it.

Erik doesn't really mind, but still, he doesn't want to go bald, however hot this bossy version of Oskar is. The one who pushes Erik's head down so he can fully slide his cock into Erik's mouth.

Oskar's big. It's not comfortable, but fuck, it's mind-blowingly awesome and so freaking sexy, the way he just loses the plot. His hips jerk and his legs kick out as Erik slowly starts to bob up and down, using his tongue to create friction. He doesn't want to stop, so turned on by the helpless desperation in Oskar's body.

Up, down, up—he licks the head as he comes off and then takes him all the way down in one steady stroke, and Oskar roars above him, shakes and shouts and tugs at Erik's hair to the point that it's a little bit painful, but Erik no longer cares. He's very, very hard, and if he leans his shoulder just so, he can keep one hand on the base of Oskar's cock and with the other hand work his own desperate length.

Oh yeah. Here we go. Much better.

He swallows Oskar down and starts pumping in time with his mouth, slow and steady at first, sucking around the tip, then moving faster, the familiar feeling rushing closer as Oskar gets louder and louder, tugs and pushes and shouts that he loves him. At least, he thinks that's what Oskar is shouting. It's a bit hard to hear with the sensations rushing through his head, of blood pumping and the slap and slurp of his lips as drool escapes and dribbles down his chin, the salty taste on his tongue and Oskar's scent, all musky and soft and—

"Stop!" Oskar shouts and pushes Erik's head away.

He sits up, all wild and glassy-eyed and his cock wet from spit, and Erik wants to eat him up. Kiss him and touch him, and fuck, *please let me suck your cock again.*

"I want you to fuck me." Oskar looks determined. Perhaps slightly unhinged, but very determined.

"We don't have to do everything in one night, baby. It's a big thing to have anal sex. Not everyone likes it, and I don't want to hurt you. We can take it slow. We've got loads of time—"

"No!" Oskar shouts. "A bomb could drop on us tomorrow, or some terrorist shit like that, and then we'd die without ever knowing if we like it, and I want to have proper sex with you. I want to feel what it's like to have you inside me. I want to be yours. I want to be the one to have sex with you. I want to be the only one you ever have sex with. Because you're mine. Mine. I want to make sure. I want—"

"Shhhhh, baby," Erik coos, and he is all over Oskar, crawling on top of him, kissing his face and kissing that mouth of his, which is still trying to speak. "Just relax and let me make you feel good. Whatever you want, I will give you." He kisses him again and rests his forehead against Oskar's. Just breathing.

"Then do it. Fuck me. I know I can take it. I've played with myself before. You just need to loosen me up a little." Oskar is slurring like he's drunk.

"We didn't buy any lube or condoms." Erik kisses him again.

"I might have some," Oskar whispers and hides his face in Erik's neck.

"What do you mean, you *might* have some? Baby, you either own condoms or you don't."

"I did a clinical trial for Professor Reinback's dermatology class." Oskar wraps his arms around Erik's body, tightly, as if he's expecting Erik to flee. "I was testing stuff for this Latex-allergy alternatives study. I have a boxful under my bed. I was supposed to hand them out to people and then ask what they thought and if they had any reactions to them, but I… I cheated. I just made it all up for my report. I never used any of the stuff."

Erik's mouth hangs open. He's truly shocked Oskar would do something like this, but then he laughs. "You naughty little minx," he says, his head already over the side of the bed, hands tugging at a cardboard box stuck under the frame.

"I cheated and still got the extra credit," Oskar says miserably and rolls onto his stomach, stuffing his face in the pillow. "I've never cheated before, but I just couldn't do it—go up to strangers and offer them condoms."

Erik sits up with the open box on his lap. "Whoa!"

"What?" Oskar doesn't even look up, his face still buried in pillow.

"Cock rings? Seriously, Oskar? 'Astroglide Light—super-smooth, latex-alternative, extra-strong condoms for sensitive skin'? We're going to have *so much* fun. It's like fucking Christmas in a box."

"It *is* Christmas, you prat." Oskar laughs into the pillow.

"I know." Erik throws himself down next to Oskar and kisses his shoulder. "Look at me," he says, and Oskar reluctantly turns his head. "You want to do this?"

Oskar nods. "I really want this."

"This being…?"

"Just you and me and…oh, fuck you. Don't make me say it."

"We don't have to—" Erik starts, but Oskar smashes his hand over Erik's mouth.

"We do," Oskar says. "*I* do."

"Always so bossy," Erik mumbles under Oskar's hand. Oskar moves it away, replacing it with his lips.

"Do it," Oskar murmurs, and then his tongue dives into Erik's mouth like it's dessert.

Oskar is all over him, one minute straddling him, the next, full-body-writhing. He's like a kid on Christmas morning again, playing with his new toy but not knowing where to start. Erik doesn't have the heart to slow him down because in all his uncoordinated glory, Oskar is like no one else Erik has ever seen. He's doing this. All in.

Oskar licks lines down Erik's chest and sucks bruises into his hipbones while his fingers play with Erik's cock, soft strokes that have Erik whinging in frustration and thrusting his hips up from the mattress. Begging.

Please. Just touch me and give me what I need.

In an attempt to keep still, he clumsily rests his hands on Oskar's shoulders as Oskar bends down to deliver little kisses, licks and sucks to Erik's cock. Erik can't help it. He thrusts up again, and Oskar's hands slide underneath him to knead his buttocks as Oskar's mouth wreaks havoc down the insides of Erik's thighs. He'll be covered in bruises tomorrow; blotches of red already mark Oskar's trail of destruction down his chest, and Erik loves it. He loves the way Oskar is rough-housing him, tugging at his hips to get a better angle, licking under his balls and…he's fucking going there, Erik realises with a needy grunt as his legs are pushed apart.

"Lube," Oskar demands from his place between Erik's thighs, and Erik grapples desperately in the box, sachets and bottles falling to the floor as he tips the whole lot out onto the bed and hands Oskar a bottle.

"You're going to do me?"

"What?" Oskar murmurs without letting up, and Erik grunts again at the hot pressure as Oskar licks a line along his taint.

"I thought you wanted me to fuck you. Are you fucking me instead? Is that what we're doing?"

Fuck. He thought this was something he might not be into. He's seen porn, okay? He knows what this entails, and the idea of it is hot as fuck. But the reality? Awkward.

"Would you let me?" Oskar whispers, his face all flushed as he pops up between Erik's knees.

Erik's legs clamp around Oskar's head. He can feel Oskar's fingertip pressing, and there is slippery lube dripping everywhere, and then Oskar shuffles up, and…*fuck.*

He has been blown before, not that he remembers much more than having a wet, hot mouth on his cock, yet right now, he feels like a bloody virgin on his wedding night because Oskar's mouth is something else. He might be a bit heavy-handed with the kissing, but fucking hell, he knows his way around Erik's cock. In fact, Erik's beginning to think he might be the one who needs lessons.

"You can do anything…to me," Erik grunts, finally, in answer to Oskar's question, too confused to figure out what he actually means. "Whatever you want…just do it." Immediately, his brain starts to backtrack, wondering if it might be better to call a timeout, but then Oskar's mouth pops off Erik's cock, and all his rational thoughts evaporate as the need for more once again scrambles his brain.

"Okay?" Oskar asks, his voice all gravelly.

"You need to teach me how to do that, it feels bloody amazing." Erik almost howls as the tip of his cock hits the back of Oskar's throat. Then Oskar swallows…or something, and explosions go off all along Erik's spine, and his legs go up in the air, and *fucking hell, is that a finger up my bum?*

He has no idea if he's howling or just kind of drooling and

spluttering out spit because something that feels this weird can't possibly feel amazing at the same time. But it does. Oskar's finger moves in and out, a slow, gentle motion in time with the indescribable, torturous acts his mouth is committing against Erik's cock.

Erik rolls, with Oskar still attached to his cock, and Oskar pulls out. Then there is this delicious pressure as he sticks his finger back in. Fingers? Whatever, the fireworks along Erik's spine have just about doubled, and…yeah, there's definitely more than one finger up his arse, filling him, but still he wants more. It's weird, and maybe it's not entirely painless, but it's sexy as hell, and he can't believe he's even thinking it.

"Do it!" he shouts.

"Do what, baby?" Oskar sinks down onto Erik's cock again, and Erik groans loudly, startling himself with how vocal he is in bed. He's never been like this before.

"Fuck me!" he roars, pushing Oskar off him and rolling onto his stomach. His legs feel like jelly, and his body is full of something he can't quite explain, like he's on drugs or has the sugar rush of the century.

Oskar kneels on the bed, staring as if Erik has completely lost his mind. It's true. He's behaving like some kind of sex-deprived slut, shamelessly sticking his arse in the air, his face buried in the pillows. He promised Oskar he'd fuck him, yet here he is, stealing the show, being selfish and arrogant and needy and…*fucking hell*.

It's even better like this, with Oskar on his knees behind him. His fingers go even deeper, and *yes, yes, yes, yes, yes*…when he gets the angle just right, it's like nothing else.

"Oh, *fuck*. Oh, yes."

"Is that it?" Oskar asks, his voice full of awe. "Is that your prostate?"

Erik would reply, but he's kind of seeing stars.

Then Oskar pulls out, and Erik whinges like a baby, begs and whimpers until Oskar is back, and something presses against him, and…*there it is. The pressure. Fuck. Shit.*

They weren't kidding. It's uncomfortably weird and stretching his skin, and the sting is unreal. His body tenses, his spine arching of its own accord, and Oskar's hands are all over his back, soothing him.

Please stop, yet fuck, please don't stop, because…oh god.

Erik can't even think. It's just. *Oh. Oh god.*

He can't believe he's doing this.

Maybe he should have been clearer.

Maybe he should have asked Oskar to prepare him better.

Maybe he should have said no.

"CONDOM!" Oskar shrieks and pulls out.

"GET THE FUCK BACK IN THERE!" Erik shrieks back.

"Need a condom!" Oskar scrambles desperately across the bed, trying to rip open a box with his teeth.

"FUCK THE CONDOM! You're already in there, and we fucking won't need them!"

"I'm a fucking virgin," Oskar provides desperately.

"I give blood. I get tested every three months, and I haven't had sex for over a year. Get the hell back in there!"

"Why are we shouting?"

"I don't know! You're the fucking doctor! Now fuck the hell out of me before I slam you down on this bed and fuck you instead."

"Bloody bossy, you guys upstairs," Oskar snarls.

Erik pouts and pushes his bum back up in the air, then kind of loses his mind as Oskar pushes back in, his cock wet with more lube, and it's bloody amazing. Slick and hard and filling him up, making his body shiver with need. Oskar grips Erik's hips and thrusts. Hard. Pulls back out and pushes back in.

Erik's not ready. He's nowhere near ready. It's hard. It's a little bit…*oh, fuck. It hurts. A little. But it's…*

Yes.

There it is.

Oh, yes.

❄

Oskar can't understand how he didn't know. How he has gone for so long without this amazing thing the world raves about.

Sex.

Because it's *fucking awesome*.

He tries to bend over to get to Erik's lips, but Erik's too tall and Oskar is too bloody short, and anatomy is an awkward thing because he can't reach anything, however hard he tries to slam his hips against Erik's arse and still keep his grip on Erik's cock, which is coming back to life in Oskar's fist.

So, he forces himself to pull out and flips Erik over.

Erik looks completely lost. Gone. Eyes closed and panting, his face is all red and his hands are shaking as Oskar pushes his legs up in the air.

It's undignified at its best, but Oskar needs this. He loves this. He needs this to be perfect and doesn't care if it's not the way it should be done. He just wants to love Erik the way Erik deserves to be loved. This is the only thought on his mind as he lines himself up and pushes back in.

And it's even better this way, with Erik slowly pumping his cock between them, and Oskar can bend far enough to smash his lips onto Erik's mouth, and *yes. This is more like it.*

Oskar shifts with every thrust, trying to get the angle right, his fingers grabbing at Erik's hair, his mouth licking and sucking and kissing and tasting while his mind is smothered in fog.

He can't think anymore, hear anymore, see anymore. The world just disappears as his vision turns black. Black and ethereal and covered in stars.

He's coming. He's coming with Erik shouting into his mouth and his hands spasming in their vice-like grip on Erik's hair, and he roars. Roars into thin air as his body seems to dissolve into nothing.

There are a million things he needs to say. A million things and no words.

He collapses, still and breathless, his already softening cock sliding out of the man underneath him.

"I can't feel my legs anymore," Erik mumbles as Oskar lands on top of him.

❅

Erik pants. Totally out of breath. In awe. Because that? That was fucking unreal.

"I thought I was supposed to fuck you," he manages to whisper into Oskar's ear as the world comes back into focus and his body finally comes back under his control. He lifts his heavy arms and wraps them around Oskar's back.

"Funny, that," Oskar whispers back. "I thought so too. Think I got a little bit carried away. I feel cheated now. You promised."

Erik giggles, drunk on sex, and wraps his arms tighter around the dead weight that is post-climax Oskar. "Give me a few minutes and I will rectify that."

Oskar loosens his grip on Erik's hair, the fingers softly twirling through the strands. "We have the rest of our lives," he says. "But we're definitely doing this again."

"Hell, yes!" Erik pushes Oskar off him. "You weigh a bloody ton, baby."

Oskar flops onto the bed, his arms out like that stick-insect snow angel, as Erik gets up and stumbles to the bathroom, bringing back a glass of tap water, which Oskar gulps down in one go.

"Need to go check on Naomi," he says, getting up. He's not quite steady on his legs.

"I still have your dressing gown upstairs. Sorry about that."

"S'okay. Got a new onesie to use now." Oskar laughs and unzips his bag.

Erik grins and throws himself back on the bed. "Love you in that onesie. Makes you all soft and snuggly."

❆

Oskar closes the door behind him, zipping up his onesie as he tiptoes down the corridor. The kitchen area is deserted, the table bathed in the soft glow from the fairy lights in the window.

"They've done as they were told," he muses aloud. The table is wiped clean, and the chairs are stacked neatly. There are voices coming from Carolina's room and laughter echoing along the corridor as Oskar pushes down Naomi's door handle.

In this Bed of Snowflakes We Lie

He hopes she's asleep.

He hopes she's feeling better, now she's back in her own surroundings. In her room full of calm and the books she loves and the inspirational quotes on her wall that she carefully pins to the wallpaper.

He moves quietly and pauses to glance around the corner so as not to startle her should she be awake.

The bedside light is still on, just the way she needs it to be. She can't stand the dark. The dark brings the demons back into her head. In the light, things are more peaceful and calmer, she always says.

She's still curled up in a ball, her back flush against the wall, but her breathing is soft and steady, her hand in Victor's. He's lying next to her on the bed, his body angled around hers, like he's shielding her from the outside world.

Oskar thinks it's beautiful. He shakes his head and smiles. He never used to be like this—all romantic and sappy and full of Christmas feelings and love and warmth.

It's only been a handful of days, yet his reality has been turned on its head, changed irrevocably. Things will never be the same again; he knows that now. He will never step back, never again feel like his life is worthless.

And he will try to be a better person. To see the people around him and maybe give something back instead of hiding. Because there are good people here. There are people who are kind. Giving and helpful.

Oskar has always had the mindset that the world is against him. That people are mean and thoughtless, and he just isn't strong enough to be someone who matters.

Yet now he accepts he was wrong. He has mattered all along. It just took a ridiculous boy to fall in love with him to make him see it.

He closes Naomi's door carefully behind him and tiptoes back down the corridor to the safety of his own room, the warmth and the soft light from his bedside table, the smells softly lingering in the air, scents of sweat and bodies. *This is what sex smells like*, he realises, which makes his cock swell as thoughts and memories rush through his mind.

Because there he is. His Erik. The boy who loves him and whom Oskar loves more than anything in the whole world. On his back with his arms slung over his head, his mouth half open and his eyes closed as his little snores echo through the silence.

My Erik. My man. My boyfriend.

Oskar lets his onesie fall to the floor and digs around in his bag for his sleep clothes. It's a bit cold, and Erik is sprawled on top of the duvet, all arms and legs and hair and gorgeousness.

He needs his sleep. He needs to rest because there are just so many things they need to do. Erik has a party to pull off. Oskar has his genealogy paper to write.

They have a box full of condoms and lube.

And they have each other.

And for the first time, Oskar falls asleep thinking that things are looking pretty good. He's excited. *Bring on the party*, Oskar thinks. Kisses at midnight with the sky full of fireworks. Sleeping here with Erik in his arms. Every single night. Bring on the sex. Bring on new friends and new beginnings.

Bring it on, Oskar thinks.

Then he doesn't think anymore.

TWENTY-SIX

By New Year's Eve, life is back to normal. Oskar is flat out in his bed watching Netflix, the pillow next to him empty and cold. He's spoken to his parents, exchanged the customary greetings and answered the obligatory questions with the appropriate answers.

He's a dick; he can freely admit that to himself. It's just not his thing, and the very thought of going to the party of the year—which may have been the brainchild of his boyfriend and taken months to plan. The party that Erik is really proud of, where everyone will be there cheering him on—has him reverting to his pre-Erik, anxious self. Because he is who he is, and he's not like everyone else.

Nor is Naomi, who appears in the doorway, quiet as a mouse.

"Don't you knock?" he asks, not that he really minds. But hello? Rules? He's sure—pretty sure—his door was closed.

"Oh, pack it in, Oskar, it's just me." She plonks herself down at the end of the bed. "How are you?"

"I'm fine." He huffs out a deep breath. "All fine. I just want to lie here and watch this…" He waves at the screen in front of him. "Whatever it is."

"It's okay not to do what everyone else does. You know that, don't you? Just because Erik tells you to do something, it doesn't mean you have to do it."

Oskar shouldn't laugh when she looks so concerned for him, but he can't help it.

"Erik doesn't tell me what to do. I'm my own person, and before you have a go at me, I'm not going to that shitty party."

She rolls her eyes and does that smile she does—the one that says *you're ridiculous*. He knows he's ridiculous. All the time, it seems.

"I'm going to make soup," she says. "Do you want some? We could light candles and sit out in the common room for a bit?"

"Isn't Victor with you?"

Damn Victor hasn't left the downstairs dorms for days, always there like a sticky plaster, staring at Naomi as if he expects her to shatter into dust if he isn't around to prevent it.

"Of course he is. He's popped over to the party to help out with something. He'll be back."

"Cool," Oskar says and stares at the screen. He can't even remember what he's watching.

"You know I'll always be here for you." She shuffles closer and pats his leg, trying to catch his eye as she keeps talking. "Even if you pretend to ignore me and sulk because I haven't been around much this week. I'm always here for you and you're my best friend, I mean that. I've never met anyone who's been as nice to me as you have. You understand me and help me. You're always here when I need you, and I love you for that. You've made me realise that it's fine to be broken. We're all broken in one way or another, but we can still live our lives and even be happy. We can find those small glimpses of good times, you know? Even when things are dark, sometimes things are really, *really* good. You taught me that. Remember?"

"Yeah." It makes him smile, the bullshit he's come out with to make her feel better. But it's kind of true. There have been good times. Some *really* good times.

"Remember when we passed our first exam?" she says. "Everyone here was drunk, and you and I went out and sat on that park bench and ate an entire tub of ice cream?" She smiles, gently rubbing his legs through the duvet.

"Yeah. Then we both felt so sick afterwards. I haven't eaten ice-cream since. But it was a good night. Just you and me and the stars."

"And two litres of raspberry ripple."

"Yeah."

"I'm going to go out to the kitchen and make that soup now. Feel free to come join me if you need me. Otherwise, I'll leave you to yourself. You're okay, aren't you?" She still looks concerned, despite the smile on her face. "Everything is good, right?"

"Yeah." He smiles. "It's all good."

"You know you were invited—we all were. They want you to be there. You do know that?"

"Night, night, Naomi. Happy New Year." He's being a dick. Again.

"I'll leave you in peace," she says. "Happy New Year, sweetie."

The door clicks, closing behind her, and he lets out the breath he's been holding. His shoulders relax again. Just him. On his own. It's…

Okay, it's not perfect because Erik isn't here, and Oskar's stomach hurts when he lets himself think about it all.

Everyone is out there, celebrating the end of another year, while Oskar is lying here trying to justify his shitty behaviour.

Erik doesn't deserve this. He doesn't deserve Oskar's pathetic panic-stricken moments of self-doubt that led him to throw a brand-new jumper—one he picked out himself—in the bin instead of getting dressed and taking the ten-minute-or-so stroll to the building where the student party of the year is taking place.

Erik.

Fuck, he loves Erik so much that it's paralysing, leaving him in a sweat-drenched heap of hope that Erik is having a good time and will forget Oskar exists. The sheer thought of leaving the safety of his bed right now and going to that party makes Oskar want to fold in on himself with fear. Loud music and people and dancing and drinking and strangers and expectations and everyone looking at him wondering why the hell he's there. He never goes to these things. Ever.

Erik said it was okay, that he would miss him and there was nothing he wanted more in the world than to have Oskar in his arms at midnight, but he was the host and organiser and had to be there to supervise the fireworks and changing over the beer kegs and toasting and all the other stuff that goes with a party. The music curfew and making sure no alcohol is served after one a.m. and that the hall is emptied, cleaned and secured in time for the patrol at three a.m. It's all Erik's responsibility. He needs to be there, and somewhere in the back of his mind, Oskar accepts he should be there too, supporting Erik.

He does a silent scream into the room and throws off the duvet, staring in dismay at his pyjama-clad legs. He was going to put on the cat onesie, to try to make himself feel better, but the minute his fingers touched the soft, plush fabric, he freaked out.

He's a shit person. A *shit* person, once again letting his fears control his life when his heart belongs to Erik. It should be strong enough to be right in there, beating the shit out of his fears. But it's not. It's not enough.

Which means he falls back onto the bed with a not-so-silent scream.

"Dude." The voice outside the door is kind of harsh, even though it's Mathias, and he's a nice person. Or was, seeing as people are supposed to knock and wait, but Mathias knocks and opens the door at the same time, and then just walks in and plonks himself down on Oskar's chair like he owns the place.

The way Erik does. They are truly all cut from the same mould, those boys upstairs.

"Dude…" Oskar whines.

"I know what you're doing, and yeah, Erik told me not to come get you, because you have some kind of messy anxieties about parties and things, which is, like, totally unfounded, but, yeah, I can respect that."

He's confusing, Mathias. Always talking with lots of extra words thrown in that make very little sense, yet he's honest and speaks his mind. Says a little too much at times, but Oskar likes him. He likes all of the guys upstairs—he thinks. He's barely spent any time with them, but they greet him with high-fives and hugs and treat him like he's one of them.

"I just don't like parties." Oskar sounds like a child, whining and whinging, and he really doesn't want to go to this bloody party. Can't people just leave him the fuck alone?

"This isn't about the party," Mathias says sternly, leaning forward and planting his elbows on his knees. "I don't give a fuck about the party. To be honest, I'd rather be with my girlfriend, but she has a family thing and I wasn't invited, which kind of sucks, yeah? So, here I am, making the most of it. And it's a good party. It would be even better if Erik smiled once in a while. Do you see what I mean?"

"No," Oskar says stubbornly.

"You're a dick," Mathias says, and he means it.

"I know," Oskar whispers.

"Yeah. You are. I should be grinding on the dance floor with my free beer, not sitting here getting pissed off at my best friend's boyfriend, who should be at said party holding his hand and making him smile and giving him smoochy kisses at midnight."

"He's busy, and I'd just be in the way, and then I'd stand there like an idiot and not know what to do."

"Hell, no! You'd be out on the dance floor with me, I could show you off and teach you some moves. The girls would love that, and let me tell you, there are some *hot* girls at that party. Not as hot as my Ruthie, mind you, and you're not into girls, but…yeah. Imagine—you and me grinding to some beats and Erik getting well-jel and coming to drag you away. See what I mean?"

Oskar does, and the whole scene playing out in his head feels like something out of his worst nightmares, as he grimaces and Mathias just keeps talking.

"Right now Erik is stood there in his poncy suit looking a million dollars, and all he does is stare at his phone, hoping you'll turn up. You know, he's really touchy-feely, Erik. He needs lots of hugs."

Mathias lets out a resigned laugh, like he knows he's hit a dead end, but then adds, "Erik loves you," and his whole demeanour changes from pissed-off cool dude to someone far older and more serious. "Oskar, he's not made of stone. Deep down, he's really insecure and scared. I know because I talk to him. He's not at that party to get drunk and score. He's there because this stuff—organising big parties and getting people together, and, yeah, basically making people happy—that's the shit he's good at."

"He's a people person," Oskar says.

"Yeah, he is," Mathias agrees. "He's also someone who loves you. Do I have to say it again?"

"No." Oskar shakes his head. "I know."

This is getting awkward, with Mathias sitting there in his suit and Oskar splayed on the bed in his sleep gear.

And the uncomfortable truth that is like a giant white elephant in the overcrowded room.

"Do you love him?" Mathias asks.

"Of course I do!" Oskar can't keep the irritation out of his voice.

"Good answer. If you'd said that you didn't, I'd have to give you a lecture on being the shithead of the century."

"I love him," Oskar snaps. "So shut up."

"Then why are you not plastered to your boyfriend's side, hugging the shit out of him and kissing him at midnight?"

"I don't know!" Oskar shouts like a petulant child. *Fuck.*

Mathias sits back with a devilish grin on his face. "I used to be just as scared as you, you know. In my last year of school, I became the ugliest, shyest, little nerd of the century. I had the *worst* haircut and a face only a mother would love, and guess what? Even my mother didn't get to love me because she died from bloody cancer when I was ten. My dad raised me, and we spent all our time being sad and depressed on the sofa. So you see? I wasn't always like this."

For a minute, Oskar stares at Mathias like he's speaking Mandarin and Oskar doesn't understand a word of it. Then he finds his voice again.

"Sorry about your mum. That must have sucked. What changed, though?"

Mathias shrugs. "I moved in here, and there were these guys who looked like some kind of supermodels and all wore cool clothes, and there was me with my cheap supermarket tracksuit and a sleeping bag and nowhere to run, nowhere to hide. I spent the first month locked in my room. Worst month of my life."

"Why—" Oskar stops. It's a stupid question. He knows why. He spent his first month at university pretty much locked in his room, wondering if failure was an option and if he should just give up and go home.

"Why? Because I spent my entire life being bullied and ignored, and things kept going from bad to worse. Here I was at uni, in the wrong dorm because obviously the dorm up there—" Mathias nods towards the ceiling "—is the cool dorm, and I belonged in loser alley. Some basement dorm where the misfits and nerds live. I didn't belong, and I was shit-scared. I wanted to kill myself at the beginning of week three."

"No! Don't joke about shit like that."

"I'm not joking. It was the worst month of my life."

They sit there in silence, the room eating up the oxygen as Oskar's stomach churns because he knows Mathias isn't done yet.

"One day, Erik caught me sneaking out of my room and dragged me into the common room and sat me down on a chair. Then he read me the riot act, told me to stop hiding and get to know the people who would become the most important people in my life. The ones I'd remember, who would shape my future—who I would become." Mathias has to stop and breathe, suddenly looking more determined than ever.

"He said some seriously weird things about becoming an adult and being a good friend and loving your neighbour, and I remember feeling all kinds of scared because I thought he was going to beat me up at one point. But do you know what he did? He made me hot chocolate and fed me biscuits and told me that we were going to a party. And he promised not to leave my side, because he'd already been here for a year and had never actually been to a student party. That was it—the day he and I grew up and reclaimed being cool."

"I can believe that." Oskar smiles. "Sounds very much like Erik."

"I lost ten kilos in two months because I was too busy to comfort eat. I hung out with Erik and walked and got roped into playing softball and meeting people—I met some great people—and got a haircut and figured out how to be me. I'm not the same person as I was three years ago. I'm someone new, someone who is good at what I study, and I have a beautiful girl who loves me, and I get to have sex and...dude...I'm happy."

"And your point is?" Oskar asks sarcastically, but he's already lost this battle, and Mathias just laughs.

"The point is that Erik deserves to be happy too. He made me jump off a cliff, and look where I landed."

"In my room?" Oskar quips. Mathias hurls a stray pen at him.

"You're an idiot."

"I know."

"So, that's why I'm here. To make you jump."

"Jump?"

"Yep. You're going to stop being shit-scared of life, and life is going to stop sucking. Well, your life already has, you know, kind of stopped sucking, because you've found someone who loves you. See? And now you're going to go with the flow and jump off the bloody cliff and come with me to this goddamn party so you can kiss Erik at midnight and not turn into a bloody pumpkin."

"Why the hell would I turn into a pumpkin?"

"Shut up, Disney, and get dressed."

Both of them sit there for a moment, then Oskar bursts out laughing.

"Do I have a choice?"

"Nope. I have exactly one hour and forty-six minutes to keep annoying you with the shitty stories of my previous shitty life. Take your pick. Get some bloody clothes on and let's go dance or stay here and I'll bore you to tears."

"I don't own a suit," Oskar protests, but he's already on his feet as Mathias slowly rises from the chair.

"Do you honestly think Erik cares what you're wearing? He just needs you there to tell him you love him. Those three small words that will make him the happiest man on earth. If I could be with my Ruthie and tell her those words right now, I would. But I'll speak to her at midnight, and she'll probably cry, and I'll bawl like a baby and snot all over this fine suit. We all have our moments."

"So…I'm going to this party?"

"Even if I have to drag you there, and you and I are going to dance, and nobody is going to care, and then we're going to have fun and you're going to kiss my best friend, because he's bloody awesome and I need him to smile. It's New Year's Eve, and everyone should be happy. Especially Erik."

They stand in awkward silence again, but only briefly, as Mathias reaches out and grabs Oskar and hugs the shit out of him. Oskar squirms, his brain insisting he doesn't do these kind of hugs while his body betrays him and hugs Mathias back and laughs even though Oskar doesn't want to, and finally relaxes as Mathias releases him and playfully swats him over the head.

"Get fucking dressed, Disney. We have a life to live. Nobody's spending the stroke of midnight alone this year. That's my mission, and I don't abandon a mission once I start."

"I can kind of see that," Oskar says as he fishes the damn jumper out of the bin.

"This okay?" he asks. He's not sure why. Mathias just rolls his eyes.

Oskar gets dressed—jumper, slacks and a jacket—and walks out the door, laughing as Mathias loudly proclaims, "It's a Christmas miracle!!" to the silent corridor. Then Mathias stops and yanks Oskar back, shushing him.

They both crane their necks so they can peek into the darkened common room, where Naomi is moving quietly across the floor, dancing to the silent beat of her headphones. She's not alone either, as Victor's arm comes into view, grabbing her hand and spinning her around in a circle like an uncoordinated ballerina. Her laughter is soft and quiet, but it leaves a lump in Oskar's throat.

"She's happy," he whispers.

"Yeah." Mathias rests his chin on Oskar's shoulder. "Everyone deserves to be happy. And sometimes, meeting that one right person can change your life. Erik changed mine, and Ruthie, my gorgeous girl completed it. I'm happy. Life's so much easier when you're happy."

"I think you're right. It's still hard, though. Sometimes I lose my nerve."

"We all do, but we just need to remember what's important."

"You're a wise guy," Oskar says as they move off, and Naomi spins into Victor's embrace.

❄

They walk in silence through the quiet streets, where abandoned student dorms nestle side by side with quirky wooden villas and apartment buildings whose windows fill the night with Christmas stars and the dull beat of party music. The temperature has fallen again, and Mathias pulls his woollen hat over his ears as Oskar zips his jacket all the way up so he can hide his face in the collar.

"What happened to your dad?" he asks, hoping it's not too much of a personal question.

"He could have become a drunkard and ruined his life. Instead, he sent me to uni and sold our flat. Now he lives in a tiny studio and drives a long-distance lorry. He always wanted to do that and never could, because he had me to look after. Not that he blamed me, but he told me to go and figure out what to do with my life and not to settle for mediocre. He encouraged me to chase my dreams, only I didn't have a clue what my dreams were."

"Have you figured out what your dreams are now?"

"Nope. Still haven't got a clue, but I'm halfway through an engineering degree so, whatever. I enjoy it, and perhaps I'll get the perfect job and be happy. Or I might just drop everything and start driving a beast of a lorry around Europe so I can see a bit of the world. Like my dad."

"Sounds cool, your dad."

"Yeah, he is. He's happy these days, too—has a nice girlfriend and enjoys fine wine and shit."

"My mum enjoys fine wine and yoga. And more fine wine. And spa treatments."

"Rich housewife?"

"Nah. Surgeon. Earns a shitload of money and is constantly on the verge of a nervous breakdown. But she's really good at what she does, and I think she's happy. My dad, lives for his bonuses and leases a new car every year. I suppose he's happy too. That makes them sound really shallow, but honestly, they're not. It's just their lives, you know?"

"Are they good to you?"

"They're everything I need. I don't think…I don't think I'd want to change anything. Not now. Perhaps I'm kind of growing up, in some strange way?"

"You still need to grow up." Mathias laughs. "And not be a dick to your boyfriend."

"Not everyone likes to party," Oskar argues and blushes. He needs to stop fighting this corner. Because honestly, he doesn't know if it's worth fighting for.

"Everyone has a right to be who they are," Mathias agrees. "Even if you just turn up and sit in the DJ booth with a drink and read a book, Erik would be happy that you came—for him. Nobody needs to party, and yeah, we should totally respect that you don't want to come, but level with me, my man. Erik. My best friend. Your boyfriend. Totally awesome dude. We should be there for him. Am I right?"

"You are totally right." Oskar sighs, his brain finally admitting defeat. He cringes a little, knowing he's been wrong about this all along. He's let his anxieties and stubborn ideas overtake what really matters.

"Of course I am! See? Party of the century."

❄

There are people everywhere, a mass of bodies visible though the steamed-up windows of what is usually a student canteen, and flashing lights and heady beats dominate the cold air. People are stood around in the snow outside, the ground littered with bottles and cigarette stubs, a few overflowing bins by the cheerfully decorated entrance.

"We're cleaning up later," Mathias assures Oskar. "And anyway, what does it matter? It's New Year's Eve. Let's find your boy and get him kissed, then you and I are getting out on that dance floor. Trust me. I'm making you dance, and there is nothing you can do to stop me."

"Okay?" Oskar laughs and Mathias pulls him in for a hug.

"Plus I get to be Friend of the Year again," Mathias says loudly as Erik appears like an apparition, a strand of tinsel over his shoulder and a bottle of water in his hand.

"You!" he says, his face cracking into a beaming smile as Oskar dives into his arms and lets the scent of Erik's aftershave and the softness of his skin calm every fraught nerve ending.

"Sorry. Sorry I wasn't here. Sorry I was a dick. Sorry. I should have been here to help you. I was just… Sorry. I'm here now, and I'm going to kiss you at midnight, and I love you."

Erik laughs. "What?"

"I love you. You're mine, and I love you."

"I love you too. You didn't have to come, you know that, right? But fuck, you've just made this party a million times better. You want a drink?"

"Water?"

"Or beer or house wine? Or there's some sickly-sweet cocktail thing?"

"Water is fine," Oskar says and kisses Erik's cheek.

"Come over here for a sec," Erik murmurs, dragging Oskar along behind him, treading through the snow around the back of the building, where the snow is still untouched, glistening in all different colours from the lights coming through the windows. "I love when it snows like this," he says and swirls around in a circle like he's dancing an uncoordinated waltz, arms flaying and head tipped back as the snowflakes land in his hair.

"Look." He sticks out his tongue, catching a showy flake on the tip. Oskar laughs.

"You'll catch a cold, wearing just a suit out here."

"You sound just like my mum. Come, baby. Come lie with me." Erik falls down in a heap of snow, laughing as his hands fly up in the air. "Fuck, it's cold!"

"We'll get wet!"

"Don't care. I just want to watch the snowflakes."

"You and your bloody snowflakes." Oskar chuckles as he joins Erik in the snow, who's already stretched out, moving his long arms and legs slowly to create what will no doubt be a perfect snow angel underneath him. There is cold and wetness creeping through Oskar's trousers as he takes his place next to Erik.

"I promise not to recite poetry to you."

"You can do whatever you want," Oskar whispers as he looks up at the flakes hurtling towards the ground, swirling in mesmerising patterns above him.

"It's the perfect night. We've got these amazing fireworks organised for midnight, and I'll…I'll get to watch them with you."

"I'm sorry I didn't come earlier."

"Doesn't matter. You're here now, aren't you?"

"Yeah."

Oskar lies there, watching Erik watch the falling snow. The air is once again full of music and laughter, singing and shouts of joy coming through the open door from which people spill out to have a smoke or catch their breath. It must be stifling in there, hot and sweaty from bodies, the air thick with…Oskar can't find a word for what he's trying to describe. It should scare him, the thought of being inside, being part of this, but as Erik's hand finds his, tangles their cold fingers, Oskar isn't scared at all. After all, Erik is here, and he belongs with Erik. Erik, who will come home with him and kiss him good night and sleep tangled up in his sheets.

Oskar grins. Grins until his cheeks ache, both from the cold and the realisation of where he is and what he's doing. *Fuck, yeah.*

"In this bed of snowflakes, we lie…"

"No bloody poetry."

"I like poetry."

"Shut up."

"Make me."

So, Oskar does. He crawls on top of the most ridiculous boy in the world. The boy with snowflakes in his hair and the smart suit and the sparking bowtie. The boy who is everything.

Everything.

He kisses him in the snow, with cold wetness seeping through the fabric covering his knees, and Erik laughs into his mouth. Oskar laughs back, and he thinks…perhaps he is happy. Perhaps this is good? More than good.

This is right where he needs to be. Where he belongs. Wherever Erik is, Oskar will be right here, next to him. Because it makes Erik happy. It makes everyone happy. It makes Oskar feel like he is flying.

Oskar Høiland is happy, and he leans his head back, cranes his neck, and catches a snowflake on his tongue.

He's happy, and perhaps that's all that matters.

EPILOGUE
A few years later

"Hi, babe, we're home!!"

"Do you always have to shout?" Emilia sighs and defiantly puts her headphones back over her head. She's smiling, though, which is a good sign. Lukas is nowhere to be found, but Lottie skips down the hallway and jumps into Erik's outstretched arms.

"How's Uncle Erik's pretty little princess today?" he singsongs in the childish voice that makes Oskar roll his eyes as hard as Emilia. Oskar raises his hand and high-fives her as he wriggles past the kitchen table, trying to reach the coffee maker that probably still houses the remains of this morning's coffee, but he doesn't care. Right now, hot, wet and strong will do the trick. Working at a hospital like the one in Moss, nobody really cares about good coffee. It might be a small hospital, but it's as understaffed and hectic as the larger hospitals Oskar encountered during his training years.

He's happy there, running his paediatric nutritional clinics, despite the crap coffee. Mostly, he's happy because he and Erik now live permanently in Moss, in the small, newbuild apartment they own with great access to running tracks and skiing in the winter. Sometimes Oskar can hardly believe he took up skiing and laughs at himself every time he sets off up the first impossible hill towards the main trail along the coast. Laughs at the memories of Einar and Leila buying him his first set of skis and trying to choose ski boots. They're ridiculous things he can barely walk in, yet they fit him perfectly once he clicks his skis into place.

Not that he'll have time to ski today, with a flat full of kids and dinner to prepare, and he's come straight from today's clinic, so his head is kind of mush.

"And did Uncle Erik's prince have a good day at school too?" Erik coos right in his ear and delivers a kiss to his cheek while Lottie —perched high on Erik's shoulders—pats Oskar on the head.

Oskar chuckles and half-fills a mug before Erik grabs the pot and pours the dregs down the sink. "That's old coffee, babe. Let me make a fresh pot."

"Doesn't matter." Oskar grimaces as another gulp of the lukewarm, bitter liquid slides down his throat.

"How was your day?" Erik asks, effortlessly setting Lottie down on her feet, opening the fridge door and handing her a yoghurt pot, not once losing eye contact with Oskar, who laughs softly at the well-coordinated action. Lottie already has a spoon in her hand.

They may not be parents, but they're bloody good uncles, especially now Holger is working full time on the North Sea oil platforms and Emmy is back on the long, arduous night shifts, despite her new promotion. Emilia comes here in the afternoons, so she can study in peace and quiet between school and her evening dance classes without having to travel all the way home, or that's what she says. More likely, Oskar thinks, now Ludwig's left home, she craves the company, and that's more than fine with him. She's fun to have around, and he and Erik always send her home with a full belly, which inevitably results in another phone call from Elise, worrying about her daughter's 'weird' eating habits.

They're not weird. She eats well, and besides, Elise is too tired to cook in the evenings. It's really no trouble cooking for an extra person when they have to feed the other two anyway.

"Glorified babysitters," Erik will mutter, but Oskar knows full well Erik loves having the kids here as much as Oskar does himself. They have a family. It might not be their own, but their flat is full of laughter, their guest room cosily cluttered with spare mattresses and sleeping bags and toys and books left behind.

"Good day," Oskar says quietly when he realises Erik is still watching him, waiting for his response. "Nothing we couldn't handle."

"We can talk later if you need to vent," Erik says, holding Oskar's gaze, making sure he really is okay. Erik's always worried. That hasn't changed at all. Always checking up on Oskar—that he's coping. Breathing. Eating. Sleeping. Not having nightmares.

He laughs and answers the barrage of questions Erik throws at him. Yes, he had lunch, slept solid last night and has pooped and passed water. He's fine. How could he not be? He loves his work and gets to make a difference to people's lives. He's a paediatrician specialising in nutritional disorders. Sure, he's still a nerd and a hopeless nutcase, but he's exactly where he needs to be in his professional life.

"Though I may have a bit of a cold brewing," he admits happily. "nothing I can't suppress with a cup of coffee and a hug."

Which, of course he gets, both the coffee and a warm hug…and hot breath against his neck and lips, and Oskar smiles into the head of hair in his face. Places a few kisses of his own on this wonderful man's neck.

His man. His Erik. Because he is his. All his. Always and forever. Amen.

"Are we actually getting fed today, or do I have to make myself a sandwich?" Emilia mutters from the table, the beat of music seeping from her headphones.

"Bloody spoilt brat, you are," Erik says, laughing.

"I made spaghetti yesterday, and anyway, Mum said I was eating here. She's not back until late tonight. They're doing these career choices evenings again, and she's pissed off because she has to hang around and deal with lots of questions."

"It's her job, isn't it? Answering people's questions?"

"Yeah, but there are leaflets, and everything is online. People just can't be bothered to look it up and expect her to stand there and recite the entire coursework catalogue by heart." Emilia shakes her head and slips her headphones back on without receiving an answer about dinner.

"What's the plan?" Oskar asks with a sigh, hoping Erik has a pre-planned, easy dinner option that he will magically slide out of the fridge and heat in the microwave.

Erik grimaces. "I got carried away with the new library brochures. They need to match the branding on the website, and the fonts were tricky as hell, so I forgot to defrost the salmon."

"We can have that leftover spaghetti," Oskar suggests, getting the answer in a resigned head shake. "You had that for lunch?"

"It was delicious. Emilia should cook more often. I liked it."

"Came out of a packet," Emilia says. "Just buy the pasta bake mix and I will cook it again."

"Okay." Oskar rubs his eyes, too tired to think. "Any ideas?" If he wasn't a sensible, frugal junior doctor with a boyfriend whose start-up company wasn't yet starting up and who still slaved away as an underpaid website designer for Moss Council, he'd suggest they go out for dinner. But he is sensible—they both are. At the same time, he's confident Erik's company will do brilliantly *once he can devote enough time to it* instead of working ungodly hours developing cheap software and meeting impossible deadlines.

"I can see what you're thinking," Erik says. "It's fine, babe. I can manage. It's fun, despite the fact that I moan about it."

"Next year, you should take some time off. Get some projects underway."

"Next year, we should go on holiday and stop you working too much." Erik taps his finger on Oskar's nose and gives him a little wink.

"When are you going to have a baby?" Lottie asks, dumping her yoghurt pot in the sink with a clunk.

"In the recycling, Lottie, please." Erik tries to sound stern, which makes Oskar snort in amusement. "Hey, I'm trying to teach her!" Erik hisses, at which Oskar explodes into a fit of inappropriate and unhelpful giggles.

"I'm sorry, but you sound so funny trying to be all stern Uncle Erik."

Erik pouts at Oskar and taps Lottie on the head. "We're going to have a baby one day, but it might not be a little baby. We might adopt a child—maybe a kid the same age as you?"

"You could adopt some hot teenager," Emilia mutters, "so I can have a new cool brother to go out and party with at the weekend." Emilia's headphones are back on before Oskar can reply.

"You already have a super-cool brother," Erik says. "I think a toddler would be good. We could skip all the nappy years and go straight into the tantrums and then send them to school." He grins at Oskar.

"I want a baby," Oskar says and pretend sulks, knowing full well that will buy him another hug and kiss. It's true. He'd love to have a baby, but bringing up kids with Erik will be perfect, whatever their age, because Erik is amazing with them.

"I'm your baby," Lottie says, clinging to Erik's leg. "I can live with you. But then I need to go home to Mummy and Daddy, because they'll miss me."

"You'll always be my baby," Erik coos and swaps Oskar's arms for Lottie, swinging her up onto his hip as he walks out of the room.

"What about dinner?" Oskar shouts after Erik and then sighs and plonks down in the chair next to Emilia's. "Emi. Help."

"Pizza?" she suggests, sliding her phone across the table. It's already open on the delivery app.

"Chinese?" he counters.

"Thai? I like noodles."

"Vietnamese. Healthier, and we had spaghetti yesterday."

"So, pizza then. We can order a Vegetable Supreme. Lots of broccoli and spinach and stuff. Healthy fibre." Her voice drips with sarcasm. They both know all the vegetables will get picked off and left on the side.

"Kebab?" Oskar tries. "Extra garlic sauce and I'll throw in soft drinks."

"Ugh." Emi drops her headphones onto the table. "I know what you're doing, Uncle Oskar. You're trying to get me to cook. Which…can be arranged for a small fee?"

"Hey, you're not bribing me again. That didn't end well last time."

"Only because you ratted me out to Mum and she was ready to come over here and give you a spanking with her softball bat."

"That would have been classed as assault." Oskar laughs. He loves when Emi gets like this, all excited, her mind spinning with some new crazy scheme that will no doubt land him in all sorts of trouble.

"Ed Sheeran," she says. "Tickets. Next summer."

"Ed bloody Sheeran? What's the point? The dude stands there and mimes with a stupid ukulele or something."

"I love Ed Sheeran. He's cool, and he doesn't mime! He controls his background music with a computer set-up. It's actually very clever."

"It's dull. I mean, why are there no musicians? Isn't that the whole point of going to a concert? To actually see a live band? Real musicians playing instruments?"

"You're so old and backwards, Uncle Oskar. *Nobody* plays instruments these days—look at Tomorrowland. It's a music festival and not a bloody instrument in sight."

"It's a *rave* festival, Emi, and no, I'm not paying for you to go there either."

"Actually, that would be *way better* than Ed Sheeran. You'd only have to pay for the tickets, and we can take our own tent. I just need the money for the ticket."

"What ticket?" Erik asks, entering the room and flopping down into the chair opposite. "Lukas is hungry. What are we eating?"

"Did he have his flu jab today?"

"Yep, he's good."

"I'm trying to convince Oskar to let me cook dinner," Emilia says with a sugary smile, "in return for sponsoring my cultural experience during my Interrail tour next summer."

"Are you now?" Erik laughs.

"She's not going to a rave festival."

"Oh, Tomorrowland?" Erik guesses. "I'd love to go to Tomorrowland. I saw some clips on YouTube. It looks insane."

"Babe…" Oskar whines.

"But Oskar said no because he's sensible, Emi."

For a second, Oskar thinks Erik's on his side, until he adds, "So we adventurers will just have to back down."

Sometimes Oskar hates his boyfriend. Sometimes he wants to bang his head into the hard surface in front of him. Repeatedly. Other times, he finds himself smiling so hard that he doesn't know what to do with himself.

Like now. Because he's already bought tickets for the bloody rave festival, seeing as Erik has been going on about since Emi first mentioned it, and no, they're not that old, even if it is the stuff of

Oskar's more recent nightmares, but…whatever. He's given up on being afraid of things.

However, they are *not* sleeping in a tent. He's booked a nearby hotel with dinner and breakfast included, because if they're going to do the festival thing, they're bloody well doing it in style.

The only thing that *is* worrying him is that he's decided to propose. At a rave festival. Which is so out of his comfort zone it's not even funny, but he can't help it these days. Like when Erik took him camping (Oskar loved every minute) and when he booked a cheap, last-minute holiday to Mallorca. (They both hated it and spent most of their hard-earned holiday in their hotel room having sex. Which neither of them hated. At all.) And, of course, when Erik had the wild and crazy idea to uproot the lives they were building in Oslo to move back to Moss. (Best idea ever. There is no denying that they both love living here.)

He loves Erik, deeply and madly and sometimes on a level that seems kind of insane. He's overly co-dependent on Erik. They both know that. And the rings have been hidden away at the bottom of his sock drawer for a year, the result of a very un-Oskar-like impulsive moment. But when he saw them at Leila's craft shop—plain silver bands with a delicate pattern, made by a local silversmith—he had just known, and apparently, Leila had too, wiping the tears from her eyes as she set them aside. The next time he visited her shop, she slipped them into his bag, and they've been in his sock drawer ever since, burning a virtual hole in his consciousness.

"So, Emilia is cooking dinner, and in return, we're paying for your tickets to a Belgian rave festival?" Erik raises an eyebrow at Oskar.

"No." He sighs back. "Emi said she wants to see Ed Sheeran. I said no. No Ed bloody Sheeran. And we're having kebabs."

"Oh! I don't like those delivery kebabs." Erik scowls. Then laughs. "Oskar, just order the damn pizzas."

"At least the kebabs come with salad."

"Who cares? We need to eat, and we're all too tired to cook. So just go with the flow, babe."

"Will you still contribute to my concert fund?" Emi tries with a wink.

Oskar swats her playfully over the head. "Nope, Em. You'll just have to work for it like everyone else. If you want to cook, I'm willing to pay you a small wage that covers shopping for ingredients and tidying up afterwards."

"I'm not your slave," she mutters.

"Not a *slave*, an *employed chef*."

"I could be onboard with that," Erik says, shooting Oskar a supportive look.

Good save. Oskar thinks. *And damn him, I love him.*

Because there is nobody else in the world like Erik Nøst Hansen. There has never been anyone else to turn Oskar's head or make him smile the way Erik does. The way he holds him at night, scratching his back when he's all tense from a long day at work. Laughing at him when he gets himself wound up by something he's read in the news. Kissing him when he loses his mind. Soothing him when life hurts. Loving him when all he can do is lie there and be loved.

"I love you," he says out loud because Erik deserves to hear it. Every single day.

"I love you too, babe." Erik smiles. "Now…one Margarita pizza, one curried prawn with extra banana pizza and a vegetable supreme calzone?"

"Lukas wants Hawaii," Emi says, reloading the app on her phone. "Do we want the free soft drink or the free tub of ice cream?"

"Is there that offer where you get potato wedges?" Erik asks, leaning across the table so he can see the screen better.

"Yup, but we need to order four pizzas to get a free side. Plus a free soft drink or ice cream."

"Oskar?"

"Whatever." He's lost this battle already, and it doesn't really matter. He kisses Erik's head in passing and heads for the shower, passing the living room, where Lottie is on the sofa, her thumb in her mouth, watching some mindless cartoon which makes Oskar smile. And can see Lukas's feet wriggling on the mattress in the guest room. He's no doubt playing something on his iPad, letting the day's stress melt away.

In his and Erik's bedroom, Oskar strips off his work clothes, letting them fall to the floor. He'll pick them up later, when he's fed and showered and rested. When he's had the chance to get his thoughts together. When life isn't so loud.

He showers, relaxing as the hospital smells and dust and cold run off his skin, towels his hair and slips into his dressing gown—the one Uncle Asbjørn bought him for Christmas two years ago, when they were all some kind of intergalactic Jedis with inflatable swords. He chuckles at the memory, tying the multicoloured, patterned belt around his stomach.

"May the force be with you, My Lord," Erik teases, planting a kiss on his cheek. "Sorry about dinner. I promise to be more organised tomorrow.

"It's not like we can't afford pizza." Oskar smiles and shrugs. "It doesn't matter. Does it?"

"Nah. As long as my Disney Prince is fed and happy."

"You haven't called me that for years."

"I know. I just thought about it, you know, when we still lived in Oslo and we were poor and saved up discount vouchers for pizza and stuff."

"We weren't poor, just kind of…"

"Bad with money?"

Oskar snickers. The two of them were *shockingly bad* with money back then, but they've done all right—scraped together enough for a deposit on their first flat and started to pay off their student loans.

"I'm so glad I had you," Erik says. "Without you, God knows what would have become of me."

"You'd have been fine," Oskar soothes, pressing his lips against Erik's.

"My Erik from Upstairs."

"My Prince Charming—stop doing that grimacing thing with your face."

"It makes me feel like I'm all twenty-something again."

"Well, you're only twenty-nine, babe. It's me that's over the hill."

"At least I pulled off a surprise party for your thirtieth." Oskar considers it one of his greatest achievements—throwing a surprise party for the man who was *the* party organiser in uni.

"It was a brilliant party," Erik says.

"All thanks to Holger and Mathias and—"

"Shut up and kiss me."

"Make me."

"The pizza's here!" Emi shouts, but Oskar and Erik stay right where they are, quietly looking at each other as Lukas runs past the bedroom door and Emi calls for someone to wake Lottie, who is apparently fast asleep on the sofa, because the pizzas are now going cold.

None of that matters.

Nothing matters.

"I love you," Erik says, kissing Oskar's lips.

"Me too."

"I loved you first."

"First one to the table gets the garlic dip," Emi tries.

"Fuck," Erik says and almost leaves, but Oskar tugs him back by his sleeve.

"Erik?"

"Emi's ordered garlic dip."

Oskar stares deep into Erik's eyes, begging him to stay, just for a sec. "Erik."

"Yes?"

"One day…one day when we decide it's right…?"

"Yeah?"

He stops and lets out a breath. *Fuck it. Who cares about music festivals and special moments and whatever?*

"Erik, for fuck's sake, just say yes."

"Yes. Of course!" Erik says, then, "What have I agreed to?"

The laughter spilling from Oskar's mouth is freeing. Soothing. Finally, the tension drops out of his shoulders. "Just fucking marry me, yeah?"

"You want to get married?"

"Of course I want to get married. You and me. Always."

"And I already said yes, so there's no way out now, is there?" Erik is smiling, that stupidly cute smile where his whole face lights up like the sun.

Oskar's insides flip-flop as he extracts the small box from his sock drawer. "Your mum had these engraved for us. I kind of picked them out in her shop, and she got the artist to, you know, fix them."

"Huh?" For the first time, it seems to sink in, and Erik has lost the ability to speak.

"They have our names inside, look. 'Erik'—this one is mine. And this one has 'Oskar' on the inside. They're handmade by a silversmith here in Moss, and I thought they were kind of cool." Oskar shrugs nervously, hoping he hasn't overstepped…at six in the evening on a random Tuesday.

"You're proposing to me, wearing your dressing gown, with rings from Mum's shop and they even have our names in them?" Erik whispers.

"Yeah?" Oskar can't help himself. He shoots off his most shit-eating grin, and Erik launches at him and tackles him onto the bed.

"I fucking love you," he murmurs into Oskar's mouth, and Oskar just laughs.

Laughs and laughs and laughs.

"And babe?"

"Yeah?"

"Yes. Yes, yes, a million times, yes."

Acknowledgements:

This story was written as a web-based Advent calendar in 2017, where I wrote and published a chapter every day through the month of December. It was a stressful experience, but it was totally worth every late, anxious hour, writing the next day's chapter, as the story just flowed, and Oskar and Erik stole my heart from the very first sentence. I always wanted to write a forced-proximity story, and this one was just a silly idea that somehow took root.

For the original story, I drew inspiration from the amazing artwork of @elli_skam on Instagram. You can find some perhaps familiar-looking scenes among the artwork on her account. She was kind enough to let me include them in the original story, and for that, I will always be grateful.

Thank you to all of you who spent that December with me, for cheering me on and laughing and giving me ideas to incorporate. A huge thank-you to all of my Norwegian friends, who had to endure a lot of questions about Christmas cakes and traditions and how to present them. I even made an almond wreath cake, a Kransekake, purely for research, of course.

Special mentions and hugs to Magni for adding about a million missing commas and for nit-picking the Norwegian parts, and to Hanne-Monica for expertly guiding me through the town of Moss and for putting up with all my questions. Big hugs to Christina and Randi who named Freddie and Victor for me.

For this re-release, the amazing Debbie McGowan took Oskar and Erik under her wing and waved her fairy godmother wand over the entire story to make sure the book became the best it could be. Alex Korent then sprinkled his own proofing magic to fix those last little mishaps.

Miriam, Lisa, Jenni, Louise, Haidee, Taru, Jennifer, Erika, Annika and Ulrika, my amazing team, thank you for hanging in there and making my dreams come true.

To Joelle Cowley, thank you for your awesome photos.

And thank you to George, my very own Disney Prince, for letting me use you for the cover.

About the Author:

Sophia Soames should be old enough to know better but has barely grown up. She has been known to fangirl over tv-shows, has fallen in and out of love with more popstars than she dares to remember, and has a ridiculously high-flying (un-)glamourous real-life job.

Her long-suffering husband just laughs at her antics. Their children are feral. The Au Pair just sighs.

She lives in a creaky old house in rural London, although her heart is still in Scandinavia.

Discovering that the stories in her head make sense when written down has been part of the most hilarious midlife crisis ever and she hopes it may long continue.

Come find me in my reader's group on Facebook, Sophia Soames' Little Harbour.

Miriam Latu is a Norwegian artist, specialising in hand-drawn pencil portraits. She works with old-school pen and paper, and more of her work can be found on Instagram @om_hundre_ar_er_allting.

SOPHIA SOAMES

717 miles

717 miles Christmas

The Scandinavian Comfort Series

Little Harbour

Open Water

Baking Battles

In this Bed of Snowflakes we Lie

The Naked Cleaner

The Chistleworth series

Custard and Kisses

Ship of Fools

This thing with Charlie

The London Series

BREATHE

SLEEP (coming autumn 2021)

TASTE (Christmas 2021)

Short stories

What if it all goes right

Viking Airlines (2021)

Honest

***

Come join my Facebook reader's group

Sophia Soames' Little Harbour

Find me on social media @sophiasoames on all platforms

Printed in Great Britain
by Amazon